NEON
JANE

MAIA EVRIGENIS

VIRGINIA BEACH
CAPE CHARLES

Neon Jane

By Maia Evrigenis

Published by

köehlerbooks™

3705 Shore Drive
Virginia Beach, VA 23455
800–435–4811
www.koehlerbooks.com

For Jean Danaë

TABLE OF CONTENTS

CHAPTER 1
Cancer Hippie

I am waiting for a copy of my heart, but there's only junk in the mailbox. Dr. Peters called four days ago to tell me I'm fine like last year and all the years before, but I need to see this for myself. I need to see my pumping heart, my heart that refuses to be anything other than average.

Anthracyclines were the last and most powerful chemotherapies I was given to rid my body of blood cancer at thirteen, specifically acute myeloid leukemia. Anthracyclines are shown to produce long-term heart defects (leading to heart failure) and are the reason for my yearly echocardiograms. I remember one of my anthracyclines beautifully. It was smooth and blue, in a thick plastic bag hanging above me on an IV pole, so exposed and sparkling in liquid form. It was a dripping venom disguised as a melted blue Otter Pop, pushing down through the tiny tube in my chest.

When the copy of my current heart arrives, I will put it in the black binder with the others, cataloging every year since 2007. I call this creation my *Little Heart Book*. I flip through it when I've gone multiple days without thinking of cancer at all, because I'm twenty-four now, and my life is very different. My *Little Heart Book* forces me to remember—and reminds me to live life the way a cancer survivor should. I'm supposed to be forever grateful and love my life for one reason and one reason alone: I don't have cancer anymore.

But I originally made my *Little Heart Book* for another reason, to show that a therapy so determined to make me different, to change my heart forever due to cardiotoxicity, has failed. Instead, anthracycline has left my heart quite boring, and I love to see myself as somebody plain.

Closing the mailbox, I hear running on the street. I turn around, and there's Jane right in the middle of it, but I'm not worried. Cars don't have any effect on her.

"Maia, hey, Maia!"

Jane really bothers me but she's hard to get mad at. She's so cute running toward me with her lanky, tween-aged body, lack of eyebrows, and neon-pink wig covering her bald head. The pink bob stops bouncing as she slows to a walk. I hear her panting change to deep, long breaths, just like we practiced.

"Jane, you're tired. Where's your IV pole?"

"Oh yeah, Maia! I'll get it so you can push me."

She wants to stand on the metal over the wheels while I run and roll her down the sidewalk.

I stare at Neon Jane and shake my head.

"I don't think so. Not right now."

I go back inside to make tea, feeling guilty for hoping that's the last I'll see of her for the day. I want to be alone in this one-bedroom house I rent in my hometown, Sacramento—me, just me and my family photos from before and after cancer, my animal figurines, my Greek tapestry of a donkey, my turtle soap dish, my orange bedspread, my pour-over coffee maker, my two hermit crabs, my John Coltrane poster, *Two Kinds of Decay* on the coffee table, my sharp cacti in the yard. It's the perfect world I've created for myself, and I make sure to keep things tidy. I've found the city and space to fight the feelings that I must become something better, that for cancer's sake, I must greatly succeed.

When the water is boiling, I choose the Canada mug and ginger tea bag from the cabinet and pour. I lie on the big orange love seat and close my eyes while it cools next to the sunflowers on the table. I breathe and remind myself, as I often have to do, that Jane is a positive force on my life. I remind myself that I am choosing her.

I will never let my Neon Jane go.

Through my thin windows, I can hear her walking back down the street. I know it's Jane by the sound. She's found her IV pole again, which she probably stashed in some bushes. She reconnected herself to it like she so smartly figured out how to do. She's pushing the pole down the street slowly. I hear its little wheels bump and crackle against the outside world they weren't made for and don't quite know how to touch.

In the morning, Jane's there with an old diary of mine. It's the green diary, when I was a sophomore in high school, about two years into remission.

She clears her throat dramatically at the kitchen table and reads out loud, "*October 7th, 2009. Dear Diary, When I see a picture of myself from 2007, I realize I used to be one of those kids on a St. Jude's commercial. I feel different than those kids on the commercial. When people watch them, they think this: 'Those kids aren't real to me.' That's how I used to be, and still am a little. We see our own life as reality.*"

I roll my eyes.

"I was so dramatic," I say.

"You totally were."

But we both know nothing's changed.

Jane reads on.

"*It's not fun going through life trying to focus on not getting sick again—when you have absolutely no control over it. Today, I pretended, like I do every day, that everything is totally fine. I'm comforted by thoughts of doing good for the world.*"

Jane has always wanted me to go work in a lab, or go to medical school. She thinks I'd be a good doctor because I know what fighting cancer is like.

"You'd be able to relate to the kids," she says.

But I would need at least twenty years of psychotherapy (plus private tutoring) before I became a doctor, because I get weird and jealous of new discoveries in oncology. When I was still living in New York, a friend sent me the first article I'd seen on gene therapy. I skimmed it on my shattered phone while I was out walking and stopped and cried in the middle of a sidewalk in the Village.

When I was fourteen, I'd let go of the neon pink wig. I was back in town after my cancer treatment at the Lucile Packard Children's Hospital three hours away, and my hair was growing back. It was only a centimeter long and looked even shorter because it grew in curly. That first day back at my 1200-person public middle school was scarier than a lot of the days I had during cancer. To go back to a school I'd randomly disappeared from the year before, and this time without hair, caused me a disgusting amount of anxiety.

Jane has trouble understanding this. I try to tell her what 2008 was like, that it wasn't cool or sexy to be alternative, hipster, or different in middle school. This was before Cara Delevingne and Emma Watson cut their hair. At Sutter Middle School, in 2008, your jeans had to be low-rise skinnies from Abercrombie & Fitch. Girls woke up at 5 AM to wash and straighten their twelve-inch hair, every single morning.

Surviving cancer as a child did not teach me not to care what other people thought of me. It did the opposite. During treatment, my body was constantly evaluated, checked, changed, tested, eyed, cared about. Talked about. Walking my middle school hallways, all I could think was *I have the shortest hair out of all the girls in this school, and everyone notices.* Because of my non-hair, I was ugly to myself, and I would have no chance at a boyfriend until it at least hit my shoulders. Later, because of the closed-mindedness of my school when it came to hairstyles, this mindset changed. I would have no chance at a boyfriend until my appearance accurately displayed my interest in one.

"Is she like, a lesbian?"—*boy at lockers*

"I don't think so. She just has cancer."—*girl at lockers*

For a few weeks, after overhearing this conversation, I deeply contemplated my sexuality for the first time. But the truth was I wasn't a lesbian, and I got bored of this self-questioning.

I didn't have cancer anymore, and saying I still did was the worst possible rumor someone could spread about me. To say that I still had cancer meant that everything my family and I had gone through the year before was meaningless, that I had never overcome what Dr. Davis considered "the most powerful chemotherapy in the world," that none of it ever stopped, that I was still constantly fighting this thing, that I would never grow up, that I would have childhood cancer forever.

But all these thoughts are pathetic to Jane. "None of this even matters," she says now, reading my mind from across the table. "You can be so petty. You need to be stronger."

"I know. I'm sorry."

"You should move back to New York and go to NYU Langone Medical School," she says. "That's what you'll do. You'll do New York with a real major this time. We can start studying together now. All you do is sit around anyway."

"That's not true."

"You're getting your life together post-college, and writing that biography of your uncle—yeah, yeah."

Our uncle, I want to say. But for someone so "strong," Jane is pretty damn slow. She can't admit, or rather just can't believe, that I am all she turns out to be.

"At least get your old job back, Maia."

"I didn't quit last week for no reason. I don't want to work at the Delta King anymore. I can't work in customer service anymore—hotel management. I just can't. It's so fake."

"Well, it's what you're good at. And that hotel was cool, right on the river. I mean, it's not what I want you to do, but it was better than nothing."

"The biography is important, Jane. What if there's something I find out about Uncle Jason's past?"

"Leukemia is genetic, not hereditary," she says. "I googled it recently, for myself in like ten years, for when I've grown up and beat cancer and want to have kids of my own."

"Genetic not hereditary doesn't make any sense, Jane. Everyone knows that's BS."

"Well, that's what they say. They're smart; they're doctors."

"You can't believe everything doctors say. You need to think about your body for yourself."

"*Ughhh*. I hate when you go all cancer hippie."

I want to tell Jane that our uncle Jason could be the only answer to cancer we'll ever have. I want to tell her that his tragic drowning at age twenty-nine could've been due to undiagnosed leukemia, that he could've been sick and passed out in the water. I want to tell Jane that if I find this in his story, our answer to *why* will be so simple—it was in our blood. We'll never have to think about the power lines above our elementary school anymore, the Wi-Fi router in our bedroom, the pesticides we ate. But I don't tell Jane any of these things, because I don't actually believe them. I write about Uncle Jason for a different reason, for what he represents in our family, for something else he explains. I write to understand an artist with a shortened timeline, and the aftermath of that. I write so I may know what it means to not come up for air.

There are so many other things I want to tell Jane, mostly about life and how I've learned to live it in this cancer-surviving body. I want to tell her she's going to get tired of living so hard, so seriously. I want to tell her that, in a way, the girl from middle school was right; I will always have cancer, and it will always have me. Even if I did tell Jane, she wouldn't believe me. She only believes in herself and what inspires her. She must, in order to survive. But when she does and grows and gets older, she'll realize that cancer is the only thing she truly knows in this world. Once she's given permission to talk about it forever, she'll see she can do nothing else but tell it, and speak it over, again and again.

CHAPTER 2

Take

Jane takes things to make her body go. She takes blood when her cheeks turn white, when she can't walk somewhere without thinking about the next place she'll get to sit down. She takes platelets when she bleeds from a rub against a door, a packaged sandwich wrapper, a nothing. These are not cuts, but clumps of red dots—blood trying to seep out of her skin. Jane's skin is like a coffee filter.

Jane never wanted to be dangerous. When she was in kindergarten, she told her teacher she wanted to be a cat when she grew up. Now Jane is a vampire, sucking other people's blood. But Jane needs it to make her body go . . . go . . . *Go. Go, Jane. Team Jane. We love you, Jane. Our Neon Jane.*

Jane gets her first period in a children's hospital. It lasts fifteen days and only stops because of what she takes. She is a thirteen-year-old on birth control pills, skipping the placebo days. Jane takes cytarabine, etoposide, daunorubicin, mitoxantrone, and methotrexate. Jane takes everything else she takes (plus her neon-pink wig) because she takes the cytarabine, etoposide, daunorubicin, mitoxantrone, and methotrexate. These are words Jane pronounces perfectly.

Everyone back home is worried about Jane, spending time on

Jane, crying again about Jane. Other people take Jane's sisters to school and to horseback riding lessons. Other people cook them meals covered in tinfoil, with instructions for reheating on the top in twisty sharpie. Other people drive Jane's youngest sister to the San Juan Bautista mission so she can take photos, build a model, and write a report. The parents are busy caring for Jane three hours away, all because Jane must take what she takes—so that her whole life can come up, so that Jane's blood will stay inside.

I woke up in my orange bed and remembered a dream from the night before. I was in the pool at my parents' house (only twenty minutes from mine now), but I wasn't a kid. My dad was there, but he said he didn't want to swim. He sat on the edge with his feet in.

There was a central line in his chest.

"Dad, where did you get that?"

"Oh, this? I got it today actually. It's just like yours. It really makes life so much easier. You know, yours is probably gonna get infected with the water."

I looked down. I felt a central line break through the scar in my chest—and saw its outline on my swimsuit.

A central line is a five-millimeter-wide tube inserted near the heart that connects to a large vein below your left collarbone. It's what they give you when you have a disease like leukemia and need long-term care, so you don't have to do something uncomfortable and stupid, like take chemotherapy through a needle in your forearm. There's blue stitching where the tube goes through you to hold it in place, and a clear bandage that covers it. The stitches get crusty—and fighting infection with a white blood cell count like yours could destroy you—so the central line is cleaned every two to three days. First, it's cleaned by the nurses, and then they'll train your mom. The disinfectant smells like oranges. To clean the tube, they use heparin and saline solution through one of the two-way spouts at the end of the line. Your dad nicknamed heparin "hep," and whenever he says it in front of the nurses you get embarrassed.

This time the nurse is using the red spout. It feels cold below your collarbone when they push the saline through the spout and into your vein. You get a chill, but you laugh and smile. The nurse says, "Feels cold, honey?" You say, "Just a bit." She connects a syringe to the cleaned spout and fills four vials with your shit blood to send to the lab.

There is a right way to wear a central line, but no one can do it, not even Jane. This is it: stand straight up with arms high in the air, tall, strong, chest puffed out, like one of those inspirational wooden angels everyone kept giving me when I was in the hospital. (I still have one of them. It doesn't match my place, it's corny, but I had to keep one.) I take the wooden angel off the shelf above the kitchen sink.

I choose a pen from the messy drawer and draw a central line through the chest of the wooden angel. I draw a tube pushing through her honored body. Finally, I've grown up to be a "cancer doctor but for kids," like Jane wants me to be. I must choose something powerful for the angel, something that will work—anthracycline, the blue kind. I watch her stand there strong while it flows through her veins on the kill. I watch her keep her arms up in the air like that, chest out, proud, unbreakable—because I want to see if she can actually carry herself like that. I want to see if she can actually stay proud with a line straight through her heart. I put her back on the shelf and wait for her to crumble, to feel embarrassed and weak. But she doesn't. She's a wooden angel. There is no limit to what she can take.

———————

I only took drugs for fun once in my life. My senior year of college, I was at a party at Lori Baker's on East 10th and 3rd Avenue.

It was May and hot outside. I walked to the party by myself with my heels in my purse. I was sick of getting ready for parties with other girls who knew nothing about me, rushing to get places in groups. I was sick of running everywhere in New York City, running away. I wanted to walk slowly, to look in the eyes of others, to reflect on the past. I wanted to be okay with myself, to not strive for the future. I wanted to be slow. I considered my walk a physical statement. But I could never master it. It's hard to walk slowly when you're done running in New York.

At Lori's, I found my friends in the kitchen making drinks. We drank warm vodka and Coke and stood around. I was not having a good time. I was never having a good time. I went outside with my friend Cat and other girls to take Instagram pictures, and then we went back inside. Everyone was taking shots and going to the street to hail cabs. I started for the door, but Cat whispered to me that her cocaine guy was on his way.

I didn't want to do coke. I knew I shouldn't make my temple body process any more drugs. I was barely taking Advil for a headache anymore.

But now that I was sure I would move home after graduation, I thought, *Later in life, I might look back and think of this night as a cool New York thing I did.* It would be radical of me, a story. And that's who I was. A story. So, I did three lines of cocaine with a rolled-up piece of paper and talked for twenty minutes to our cab driver about tennis. Outside the club, I fell and scraped my knee on a disgusting sidewalk but got up thinking, *My immune system is good enough.* At the party, I was dancing so much, and then I didn't want to be there anymore. My friend who always tried to take care of me said we should go home. She knew I wasn't just drunk.

At my place, we talked about a boy she liked and then she passed out, but I stayed up until 4 AM. I ran to the twenty-four-hour CVS across the street to buy hydrogen peroxide. Back at the apartment, I scrubbed my knee out in the bathtub. Then I sat on the bathroom floor and silently cried. I felt guilty for putting such shit into my body. I closed my eyes and apologized to myself. I told my cells that I was sorry. I thought the life I lived made surviving cancer for nothing, because look at me, I was a vegan doing cocaine at college parties. I was not radical. I was just like everybody else. I was supposed to be different. I was supposed to have learned so much—but I was just like every other college girl in New York, crying at four o'clock in the morning. I—a cancer survivor—was everyone's first cocaine story.

This was 2016, nine years after cancer. It was when I still felt that being average was the worst thing I could possibly be, before I realized that average was the only thing I needed. Three lines of cocaine, and I had wasted my life away. But look at me now, embracing a *Little Heart Book.*

There was another time I did drugs, but it doesn't feel like it really counts. It was the end of a summer in California, and I was sitting on a deck with my two friends who were both named Haley (one spelled Hailey). Someone gave Hailey a joint as a goodbye present after a summer camp, and we were all excited to share it.

I don't remember anything we said on that deck, but whatever it was was hilarious. Everything was hilarious. I was hilarious. Hailey was hilarious. Haley was hilarious. Their same-different name was hilarious. Our whole lives were hilarious. My childhood was hilarious. Having cancer as a child wasn't sad—it was ridiculous. It was ridiculously hilarious. Me thinking I could write about it was hilarious. Me thinking of writing a biography of my uncle was hilarious. Not serious—hilarious. His story was hilarious. I couldn't stop laughing on the deck that night—it hurt my abs. It hurt so much that I keeled over on the ground—it hurt me, to think about how ridiculous my life was. Then I went inside and ate everything I could find.

———————

Today Jane has a bone marrow aspiration and a spinal tap, which means they are taking a chunk of her marrow and fluid from her spinal cord to send to the lab. They need to run tests on it, to see how well she is responding to chemotherapy.

Jane waits with her mom for two hours in the pre-op room. She hasn't been allowed to eat since the night before, but she doesn't feel hungry. She plays Titanic Rescue on her iPod touch while her mom reads *Cancer's Gift*, and then it's finally time for the procedure. Nurses Sue and Connie roll Jane on the cot to the silver and white operating room, where Jane takes propofol from the anesthesiologist. It's a white, milky fluid. He pushes it through her central line, the blue spout this time. Jane immediately feels tired but tries to stay alert because whenever she takes propofol, she plays a game with her mom. Jane's mom says a secret word as the propofol settles into her system. Jane tries to remember it when she wakes back up.

"Okay, honey, the word is . . ." Jane's mom looks around the room, trying to think of something, knowing she's running out of time.

"Brown bag."

Jane laughs quietly at her mom's strange choice.

"I'll rememb . . ." Jane says, and she falls asleep.

Jane doesn't remember the secret word when she wakes up in the recovery room. The comedown is tough this time—the worst ever. Jane wakes up to the sound of her own crying, and then the beeping of the machine next to her. She's so afraid, but she doesn't know why. She's had this same procedure seven other times, and every time it's been okay. "I'm so scared, Mom, but why am I so scared?" she says, grasping her mother's hand.

"It will pass, honey. It's because of what you took." Jane takes a purple popsicle from her nurse, Kiran. Jane pukes it up ten minutes later and cries again, feeling better only when she remembers her future self, who will be strong and somebody great. Her future self, who thinks cancer is just a thing of the past.

I wonder what my life would've been like if Uncle Jason could've visited me in the hospital, if he hadn't drowned twenty-five years before my diagnosis. I wonder if Uncle Jason would've been there when my hair started falling out onto my hospital pillow during my second round of chemotherapy. Would he have helped me shave it off? Would he have brought the pictures from when his girlfriend shaved his head at Stanford? Would he have told me the story, that my great grandma made him do it?

Maybe Jason would've helped me with music. I'd started taking saxophone lessons a year before cancer. One time, when my dad came to Palo Alto to trade places with my mom, he brought my saxophone. I played "Basie's Blues," the first song in the Jim Snidero song book, over and over again on the rooftop garden of the Lucile Packard Children's Hospital. If Uncle Jason was alive when I had cancer, maybe I could've taken music lessons from him. He could've helped me improvise over chord progressions. We could've talked about my thoughts on cancer now, as an adult, as the only two people in the family who studied art in school. I wonder what he would've inspired me to take from cancer, to make from it.

This is how it would go: Jason would be visiting Sacramento from Switzerland where he would still be teaching at the Schola, the music academy in Basel. He would be at my grandparents' house. They'd still be alive, and the house wouldn't be sold. I would go over to sit outside with him, drink kombucha, and talk about life, and he would be eating a peach.

"So, what do you want from your work lately, since my last visit home?" he asks me. "Say the answer quickly, without thinking . . . ready? Go."

"I want to be as powerful as the peach."

"Keep going."

"I want my skin to fall off, and I want to drip. But I don't want to bleed out. I don't want to lose my body."

"Is that really what you want?"

He stands up. He takes a bite of his oozing peach. He looks up at the sky.

"No . . . I . . . I want to be the wooden angel."

"Better."

"I want to be as strong as the wooden angel. I want no limit to what I can take."

"That's a start," he says.

I drive back to my house, passing eight frozen yogurt shops on the way. I park on my street and check the mail. My latest piece for my *Little Heart Book* has finally arrived. I unlock the door and throw my purse and sweater on the orange loveseat. I go to the kitchen and get a black marker from the messy drawer.

In the bathroom, I stand naked in front of the mirror and look myself strong in the eyes. I look at the scar on my chest, all because I had to take what I took. So my whole life could come up. So my blood would stay inside.

I begin to draw my central line.

CHAPTER 3
Central Line

Sanitize your hands, sanitize your daughter's hands, sanitize the kitchen countertops, sanitize the kitchen table, sanitize your daughter's Nalgene water bottle, sanitize her iPod Touch, sanitize her pill box, sanitize *The Giver*, sanitize the fluffy purple pen, sanitize your daughter's diary, sanitize her toothbrush body, sanitize the knob to the bathroom door, sanitize your daughter's bedside table, lay your daughter on the flowery bedspread and sanitize the site of her central line, sanitize the blue spout and attach the tubing to the plastic ball filled with vancomycin, sanitize the vancomycin ball and wait five hours for it to drain into your daughter, sanitize the phone and watch American Idol season eight together, sanitize the remote control, sanitize the kitchen countertops, sanitize the kitchen table, sanitize the bottom of your daughter's plate, sanitize the handle to the salad tongs, sanitize the handle of the spaghetti casserole spoon, sanitize the handle of your daughter's fork, sanitize your daughter's beads and lanyard string, sanitize your daughter's instruction book, sanitize the scissors, sanitize her bedside table, sanitize your daughter's pillbox, sanitize the Nalgene water bottle, sanitize your daughter's diary, sanitize the fluffy purple pen. Cover your daughter's central line in plastic wrap and tape so it doesn't get wet with water. Sanitize the bathtub and fill it. Sanitize your daughter.

I'm washing my hands in a gas station bathroom. I'm staring at a *Fuck* carved into the mirror. They're out of paper towels, so I open the door with my sweatshirt sleeve and walk through the snacks to the car. I open its door with my left hand and reach into a bag of almonds with my right. I start the engine, look in the rearview mirror, and see Jane lying down flat in the back seat, listening to her iPod—Avril Lavigne. She's just had a spinal tap, which means fluid was removed from her spine for testing. She has to lie down flat and still, so the fluid that still remains can settle. If she doesn't, she'll get a terrible headache.

Pulling out of the gas station, the street dips. The back of my car hits the ground on the decline.

"Hey, watch it!" Jane yells, dramatically grabbing the handle above her. "My spinal fluid's rockin' around back here!"

I head onto Alhambra, passing the Greek church where I spent Sundays as a kid. I make a right onto J Street. The map tells me there's been an accident on the freeway tonight, so I take Sacramento surface streets. I'm going to my parents' house for dinner.

"She just has cancer."

I'm passing the middle school I went to when I was just a few months into remission, when my blood count was finally high enough to be out in public. I take my eyes off the road, look out onto the school's big, open field, and remember physical education. I remember the push-up test, the sit-up test, the mile test. I think about my failing scores. I think of my cancer survivor excuse.

"So, who do you like, Maia?"

There's the Big Spoon Yogurt on my right, where I used to walk on Fridays after school with the nicest group of the most boring girls. I'd had the combined English and history class with them the year before, though I was only in class for two months before I disappeared into cancer. I never properly thanked these girls for kindly taking me in when I got back.

"I bet he totally likes you too! Do you want us to ask?"

We never talked about anything serious. We never clicked like I did with Mel, my best friend at my elementary school. But I didn't want to. What I wanted was to go to sleepover parties. I wanted to get ready at somebody's house before the middle school dance. I wanted a group to sit with at lunch. I wanted to talk about my crushes.

I wanted to pretend I was a normal kid that year.

I slow to a stop for a mother and little girl at the crosswalk connecting the Midtown Taqueria and the Irish pub. The mother makes eye contact with me, smiles. The girl starts skipping forward in her orange dress. I wonder what her blood cells are like, her counts, her hemoglobin levels. I'm worried about this girl. I'm worried about her mother.

"We've found leukemia."

The hospital where I was first diagnosed is about a mile from here. It's not on this street, which is good, because I really don't want to look at it. It's somewhere to the left of me.

I didn't know leukemia was cancer. I sat on the hospital bed, confused, knowing I'd been diagnosed with a disease. I didn't realize it until two hours later, when a nurse explained it with white and red blood cells made of felt material, and brought up my future lack of hair.

"Many children like to dye it a fun color before starting chemotherapy, like neon green, or pink, because it is going to fall out anyway."

This local hospital knew they were in no way equipped to handle a childhood cancer as severe as mine, but they tried to anyway. I see now how tempting it must've been for them to work on me, how exciting it was for them to get me as a patient, to play cancer with me. How could they resist all the money from the exorbitant chemotherapy, bone marrow aspirations, spinal taps, echocardiograms, MRIs, blood and platelet transfusions, blood tests, nights in the hospital, pain medications, and ads with my bald-headed smile on brochures and flags? I see now, 4,448 days after cancer, just how much money my body is worth, just how much it costs to keep me alive.

"It was the fastest I've ever seen a heartbeat."

I wonder what those idiot doctors and nurses said to each other during my failed central line insertion surgery at that hospital, three days after they diagnosed me. I wonder how they looked at each other when they accidentally touched my heart and I went into rapid tachycardia. *"Beautiful."* I wonder what they said to each other when they accidentally nicked my left lung too, and it filled with fluid and collapsed. *"Ah, fuck."*

I woke up to my mom screaming, yelling at somebody. But I couldn't open my eyes, or move, or talk. I could only hear. I fell back asleep and woke up again, this time for real. My throat hurt from the breathing tube, but they needed me to speak.

"What do you want to do, Maia?"

The anesthesiologist had gone home. I could risk waiting until the next day for one to show, but by that time, my left lung might be too filled with fluid. It was dangerous. I could have the procedure now instead, without anesthesia. It wouldn't hurt too bad. They had something to numb the skin.

"It's your choice."

There was *fill the lung*, or there was *empty the lung*. And please tell me, who on earth, at thirteen years old, would ever fucking choose fill?

They rolled me to another room. They rubbed a numbing cream on my left side above my ribs, and my mom held my hand. They cut a hole through my side with a scalpel—which seemed like just a regular knife—and then my mom fainted, and fell on the ground . . . and then someone helped her up, and she left the room, and then they shoved a tube through my wound. I just laid there looking back down at myself . . . and then they connected the tube to my lung and started draining out the fluid into a plastic box. I held the smelly box of my draining left-lung insides for ten days, holding it close to me so it wouldn't yank on the ambulance ride to the new hospital; I'd cry from an accidental yank. I took codeine every day for the lung-draining tube, which I learned later was inserted sloppily through the budding side-breast of a teenage girl, increasing daily pain. A doctor said this while demonstrating its removal to a group of med students. He literally just pulled it out, in one quick, electric pull.

All of this happened, all of this, because of a central line insertion that never should've happened in the first place. When I checked into the Lucile Packard Children's Hospital, they said I shouldn't have had my central line placed so early anyway. I wouldn't be ready for chemo for another week and a half.

This, all of this, and a tachycardia, and now this memory on this drive, all in what Google considers a "simple forty-five-minute procedure."

———————

I'm passing Riley's neighborhood on my right in the Fab Forties—big pretty homes lined with mandatory matching decorations depending on the upcoming holiday. I can still hear it on Guitar Hero, the same song over and over again, at a sleepover at her house. I was reading a *Seventeen* magazine on the couch, waiting for my turn, not really wanting it. I didn't feel good. I was ready for the party to end. I was reading "9 Things You Should Know Before Getting Your First Body Piercing," and then the words started disappearing. I could only see 9 *Things*, and then *You Should Know*, and then,

   9 *Things You Should Know Before Getting Your First Body Piercing*,
   9 *Things First Body Piercing*, then,

9 Before Piercing, then,

9

and my head started to throb, and I couldn't take the noise anymore. I didn't even think to ask for help or tell Mrs. Miller. It's like I knew no one could help me. I just needed to lie down. I found a bed in a room off the hallway. I had been over so many times and never seen the room before; it wasn't Sarah's, it wasn't Riley's parents', so it must've been a new guest room or a room that appeared just for me, some Harry Potter shit. In the morning, everyone teased me for passing out so early. They were finishing up a pancake breakfast.

I felt terrible. I felt like something bad was happening to me, like there was something in me, me, ME, I was in me, and I needed to get out. I called my mom eight times and puked in a sweatshirt hood in the car as we drove home on Fair Oaks Boulevard.

In a nearby park a week before that sleepover, my soccer team was getting so frustrated with me.

"Maia! Faster! Come on!"

But I couldn't move faster. It wasn't that I was tired. It was that I couldn't. It's the only feeling in my life that I've never wanted to write about, the feeling of my red blood cells at a hemoglobin level of four out of fifteen.

———

"So, will you?"

I was getting asked to prom. We were in my Christian high school's parking lot on Elvas Avenue, coming up on my left, where I'd told my boyfriend to meet me after my spring jazz concert. I walked toward him with my red saxophone case slung over my shoulder. He was smiling at me, holding a huge colorful sign in his calm, kind handwriting.

"You were awesome up there," he said.

A few months before that, I was ready. "I want to tell you something that happened to me." We were sitting in the back of my house at a desk doing homework together, surrounded by binders and pens. "I want you to read my college essay, my common app essay, that will help explain it."

"I, um, Maia, I already know."

Rosario had told him, back when we'd first started texting, trying to get to know each other. He was sorry he already knew I was a survivor. He wished I could have told him myself.

But it was okay, it was all okay, because I should've known. Everybody knew—or was just a degree away from someone who knew what I was.

———————

"We were too young to go through something like that, and then go on as teenagers, go back to normalcy. There should be a manual to best friendship after childhood cancer."

My childhood best friend said this when we had coffee around Christmas last year, trying to mend our friendship. We met in the coffee shop I'm passing now, a popular chain called Temple. This location is the boring one where no one talks, right next to our old elementary school.

It sounds insane to go through cancer with someone and then to drift. It sounds insane—to have a best friend who went to see you three hours away at the hospital every other weekend, who quit her soccer team for you, and to then be cured and not know how to hang out anymore. But cancer isn't like the movies. Mel reminded me of it all. At fourteen years old, a year after cancer, I already wanted so much to move on.

———————

Pulling into my parents' house, my sisters and I are three young, un-sick kids drawing with chalk on the driveway.

"It's not a big deal, it's not like leukemia, it's not as bad as what you had."

My younger sister, Alex, was diagnosed with juvenile diabetes (type 1), the kind that kids get, the kind from a virus. Her pancreas fails to produce insulin, which you need to bring sugar (glucose) into your cells. Alex has always been private about her diabetes and the way she takes care of it. When she came to visit me while I was away at school, we talked pretty seriously about what she goes through on a daily basis for the first time. She said she always felt bad complaining to me. This was the first time I saw how destructive it is, how silencing it is, to compare our illnesses to those of others.

When my mom and dad switched places for the weekend, my older sister, Elaine, spent three hours in the car with my dad heading to the hospital, only to visit with me for a half hour, and then turn around and drive home with my mom, all the way back to Sacramento. She was a freshman in high school at the time, and Alex was a fourth grader. I remember, when both Elaine and Alex came, we took photos on the PhotoBooth app. We distorted ourselves with those bulging and convoluted filters, in hysterics.

I walk in through my parents' garage. I still have the clicker. My dad is sitting in one of the green sofa chairs my mom unconventionally placed in the kitchen twenty years ago, when we moved into this house. The new tiny kitten she found running down C Street is walking around my dad's feet, about to hop up on his lap. He stands to give me a hug that still feels somehow awkward, even after this many years of my existence. I sit at the counter in the brown stool, where I always sat in the morning as a kid, like this, across from him in that same green sofa chair.

When he was in the hospital with me on the weekends, he always wanted to get take-out. He liked the Chinese restaurant across the street. My mom didn't want us to eat Chinese takeout. She thought I should be eating healthier food during cancer. But my dad didn't think food had a lot to do with it. They fought about this a lot.

When he left to go pick up the Chinese food, I was alone in

the hospital room (but never really alone, because I always had an annoying roommate, and a bunch of nurses on the floor).

"I'll be right back," he'd say, handing me my silver flip phone.

"Make sure yours is on."

I'd have the rolling table set up for us when he got back, fully sanitized, with napkins and plastic forks. I sat on the edge of my bed, and he pulled his chair up across from me. Sometimes we ate and played Monopoly at the same time, our meals pushed to the corner of the table. I'd have the board, the top hat, and the thimble disinfected too.

One night while we were having Chinese food, I had to have a chemotherapy shot in my leg. For some reason, they needed to give it to me at that time, 6 PM. All day my dad and I were counting down to the shot, but not talking about it, even though we were both really scared. Judy, one of my favorite nurses, came in and told me I didn't have to move. I could stay where I was, sitting on the edge of the bed with my legs hanging off, as if it were the stool in my kitchen. I'd had a chemo shot in my leg before, but this one must've been a different kind. The shot hurt so much. I could feel the chemo spreading through my thigh, my insides igniting like a highly flammable material. It didn't stop spreading for a half hour, fire in my leg. During that special night playing Monopoly, I cried and shook in front of my dad; I was so uncool, lying back down in my bed and wishing my mom was there. My dad didn't know what to do. He didn't know how to comfort me. I didn't want to be crying in front of my dad. I didn't want to make him uncomfortable.

Another time I was with my dad he heard there was a jazz show in the main hospital, the one for adults. He knew I'd want to go. There would be a saxophone player.

I didn't wear the pink wig to the show. I wore the fuzzy purple beanie. He asked if I wanted a wheelchair, but I said I felt fine to walk. We went past the families passed out in bright lights on the couches to the long hallway that connects the children's hospital to the main hospital. I was so tired walking there, but I just kept moving. My dad was pushing the IV pole next to me. *You're not even pushing the pole,* I said to myself. *You're fine.* I was so upset at my tiredness. I just wanted to go to a jazz show with my dad. When we finally got there, we watched a few songs from an upstairs balcony. But he could tell I was too tired to be there. He found a wheelchair for me and rolled me home, or to my room, I mean. I don't remember anything about the jazz show, who played, what instruments, if the improvisation was good. I only remember my dad was there.

"You're here!" says my mom, picking the new kitten up off the floor who's chasing after her, swatting her ankles. "Have you said hi to the little lady yet?" she says, holding Lady Bird to her chest. I walk over and pet the kitten on her head.

My mom puts the cat down and pulls a bottle of prosecco out of the fridge. She knows it's my favorite and pours us all a glass. My dad goes outside to fire up the barbecue.

"Want to pick tomatoes for a salad?"

We walk out to her garden with a brown paper bag.

My mom always wanted to grow things—flowers, food. She said it started when my uncle Jason died. She decided she wanted a garden and lots of kids. She wanted *life* in her life. She stands barefoot with her skinny legs and Bermuda shorts in the dirt, wine glass in one hand, the other deep in a tomato plant. She's fiercely filling the bag I carry with cherry tomatoes, heirloom tomatoes, cucumbers, and peppers. She walks with me to the end of the yard to see the bees. About one thousand of them hang out outside of their green honey house, all holding onto each other, supporting each other, cooling off at the end of the day.

"What about horses?" she says. "Horses in the yard, just hanging around, walking around, saying hi to us. How cool would that be?"

Every morning and evening during cancer, my mom administered my vancomycin ball of antibiotics, which was stored in the refrigerator. It was a plastic ball filled with fluid. If it was administered too quickly,

I had an allergic reaction, so it had to drain into me slowly over the course of five hours. That gave my body time to adjust to it. My mom had to attach the ball to one of the spouts of my central line. In the morning, I'd still be sleeping. She quietly cleaned either the red or blue spout, attached the vancomycin ball, and put it in my pajama pocket so it could drain into me while I slept.

We watched the movie *Music and Lyrics* a lot. We watched it probably sixty times while I was both inpatient and outpatient. We liked it because it was a sweet rom-com, something easy. We watched it on her laptop while we had to do something terrible, like wait three hours in the day hospital for my blood and platelet transfusions. We also liked the movie *Blades of Glory*. My mom didn't care that it was rated R and I was only thirteen. She loved watching it together, this ice-skating comedy madness. She loved it so much; she laughed insanely, laughed until she cried.

My mom never expected us to fully understand each other. She didn't know what it was like to be a sick daughter, loving a healthy mother. And I didn't know what it was like, to be a healthy mother, loving a sick daughter. But we didn't need "fully." We got it—most of it, anyways. That was enough.

My mom never told me to be strong during cancer. Not once. Not one time.

"Maybe you'll write a book about what you went through someday," she'd tell me instead.

"They won't understand."

"But what if they did?"

My parents and I sit down outside to eat together. I pour us all more wine and we say cheers. We are always celebrating something.

"Would be nice if your sisters came home every once in a while, too," my mom says.

But things are different for them. They're fierce, successful, off in Los Angeles. They only call when they're stuck on the 405.

"Did you apply for the new position at the school?" my dad asks, cutting into his steak.

"Not yet, but I will. I've been working on it." But after cancer, I stopped being able to lie to my parents. "I'll start working on it, I mean."

"It'd be great for you," says my mom.

I take a sip of my wine.

"They only want me because I had cancer as a kid."

"That's not true."

"Alex thinks so too. They remember my graduation speech at the baccalaureate mass. They think I'm interesting, strong or something, a cool alum for faculty."

"But aren't you? They have a new president anyway, so she doesn't even know about you. Didn't she just say she read your articles?"

"Someone has to have told her. And isn't it kind of lame to teach at my old high school?"

"It's a job, a paying job," says my dad.

I wonder if I'll ever outgrow this idea that in certain contexts, business contexts, my childhood cancer is the most attractive thing about me. Because cancer weakens the ones who were never sick. They think you are magic. They think you can do anything. They think you have perspective. They think you could teach a bunch of high school kids something worthwhile.

My dad goes to bed, and my mom and I move to the couch. She asks me about Jason's biography.

"I interviewed Samantha the other day," I say, petting our orange cat, Honeyboy, sleeping on a blanket next to us.

"Oh, geez."

"She was so nice!"

"She was the worst of Jason's girlfriends, Maia. We all knew it.

Even he knew it. You should've heard what Grandma had to say about her."

"I liked her. She was so blunt and honest. She didn't glorify him like the others."

"Figures," she says.

I want to talk about more serious things, but I don't know how to. I'm going to make my mom upset.

"It's crazy to think that you were my age when you had to fly to Europe to bury your brother by yourself."

"Yeah," she says. "I smoked cigarette after cigarette the entire flight."

It's strange to imagine my mom young and smoking. She's the most health-conscious person I know.

"I just can't believe Grandma and Grandpa didn't go, and made you go by yourself. You had to see his body. I mean, how traumatizing. It makes me so upset."

"Well, don't be so judgmental about it."

The cat wakes up with my mom's harsh tone, stands up, shakes a bit.

"I'm not. I'm just defending you."

"No, you're not; you're judging them."

She takes a drink of wine.

"You don't know what it's like to lose a child. None of us do. You don't know what kind of pain they were going through."

―――――――――

I'm driving home on the freeway in the dark this time. Jane's asleep in the back seat now, tired from all she's been through today. The lanes are open and fast. I'm speeding, moving past everything from before in a blur. I don't have many memories here on Highway 50, but there is one that stands out to me, that I will never forget, that I can never drive on any freeway without thinking about.

It's my favorite memory.

When I came back to Sacramento for good after cancer, my mom was driving, and I was lying in the back seat. I was surrounded by all the stuff we'd accumulated during my treatment, terrified we were going to get in a car accident, and it would all have been for nothing. I was lying flat because I'd had a spinal tap two days before.

"Maia, you have to get up. I know it hurts, but it'll be just for a second. You have to trust me. Come on honey, hurry up."

And there it was, under the bridge I'm going under right now, a sign in bubble letters and colors and streamers, made by my team, my sisters, and family friends. I sat up and stuck my head out the window, leaned out. I looked up, gripping onto my neon-pink wig for dear life in the wind.

"Welcome Home, Maia."

CHAPTER 4

New Body

Last night I had a dream I was talking to my sister in the bathroom of a restaurant. She said she didn't understand how people could take care of the sick, how people could give up their lives like that. To devote themselves. Two lives gone for the sake of one.

"You're being crazy," I told her.

"When our parents are dying, you'll be the one to give up your life to take care of them," she said, washing her hands. "Because they gave up theirs to take care of you."

Then my body started failing again. It was real—there was something inside me, something bad. I couldn't stand up. We were at some kind of barn/lodge restaurant, I don't know what it was, having dinner as a family. I had a boyfriend in the dream. It was the guy who lives across the street. As we were walking out, I fell to the ground, like in the soccer game eleven years ago. I knew what it was. It had developed so quickly, maybe over the course of the meal, a white blood cell gone rogue, eating the red, gathering followers. My sister was saying, "Well if she's so serious with this guy, why doesn't he deal with it? We can leave."

My mom was next to me, and I was yelling, "No, we're not even serious. It's too early for cancer for us. We're not even officially dating!"

A paramedic came and I was still on the ground, but now I was outside on the sidewalk. The paramedic was a teenage boy in my old roommate's car with a couch in the back seat. "Lie down here," he said. And I knew I was going to die.

———————

"Rough night?" says Jane.

I'm half asleep still, feeding the hermit crabs. I turn around and look at my bedhead in the small mirror on the wall across from me.

"Appears so," I say. "Bad dreams."

I walk to the window and pull up the blinds. My neighbor is taking his trash bins to the street. He takes the newspaper out of the bright-orange *Sacramento Bee* container under his mailbox.

"Oh, my gosh, he's totally adorable," says Jane, peering under my shoulder. "You like him, right? But what about Kyle Evans?" she says.

"What about him?"

She pulls a letter out of her pocket and reads it out loud.

"Dear Jane, I hope you are having a better day today. Do you ever get to take walks around the hospital? I liked doing that when I was feeling good. I remember how hard it was to be sick. School today was pretty boring. Your friend, Kyle."

"Cute," I say.

"He just gets it."

"Gets what?"

"My leukemia."

"But didn't he have a brain tumor, or something, and end up leaving the hospital to treat it with vegan food and a spiritual healer?"

"He still counts."

"Counts as what?"

"As having cancer! I want to marry someone who had cancer as a kid, like me. I'll only gel with someone who's been sick. That's the only way I'll fall in love, if they get me."

"But love doesn't have requirements like that. You'll see."

"How would you know? It's not like you even have a boyfriend."

"Jane!"

"Just sayin', shouldn't you have a boyfriend by now?"

"I've had plenty of boyfriends."

"Well, I hated them all. They were barely real—the drummer in New York, the second drummer in New York, the hipster sociologist, the best guy friend from high school who just used you as a therapist! They weren't real; they didn't care about you. They weren't survivors."

"Boys can still care a lot about you and not want to marry you or even date you seriously. You'll date a ton of people in your life, Jane. You're just going to like them and not really know why."

"Well, I think that's stupid. I'm looking for cancer in a guy as of now, like in *The Fault in Our Stars*. Let me know if you know anybody you can set me up with—the balder the better."

I fill the kettle with water for our turmeric tea. She starts talking about what she looks for in a boyfriend as I take two mugs from the cabinet.

I listen, but I've heard it all before. I know the only kind of guy Jane wants. She wants a boyfriend who has cancer, who has a central line in his chest and a headache from a spinal tap when he sits up in his hospital bed. She wants a boyfriend who takes propofol twice a month for his bone marrow aspirations, who sleeps with a monitor clipped around his pointer finger, who wakes up to a nurse taking five vials of blood from his red spout. She wants a boyfriend whose results came back MRD positive, who can pronounce the words cytarabine, etoposide, daunorubicin, mitoxantrone, and methotrexate, who refuses to shit in the plastic bucket. She wants a boyfriend who thanks his doctor and loves his mom and replies to comments on his CaringBridge blog page. She wants a boyfriend who got a nosebleed under the power lines at his school, who slept with the internet server under his bed, who ate pesticides on his fruit. She wants a boyfriend who collapsed in his championship basketball game, who knows the proper way to breathe so a blood pressure cuff can read quickly and let go. She wants a boyfriend who has a feeding tube up his nose, who has bumps all over his lower back, who has a mouth sore and dry hands from using Purell thirty times a day. She wants a boyfriend who is balding at thirteen, wearing a neon orange wig, whose white blood cells are eating his red.

———————

I'm making a timeline of Uncle Jason's two years in Switzerland at the bar around the corner from my house, next to the soap refill place. I drink a Track 7 in a cold, tall glass and watch people play bad pool. I recognize a girl from middle school in a group that comes in, but she doesn't recognize me. I don't say anything. I just write— Uncle Jason did this, Uncle Jason did that.

I'm bored by Uncle Jason's "cool" life of travel, of getting out of Sacramento, of composing and performing, of things his smart friends said. I'm annoyed at his letters, at his "better than thou" way of talking to me, or to whomever he was writing to. I read now in his blue travel journal: *Somehow, suffering is involved here; but it is a conscious suffering, going the hard way in order to learn something unobtainable by a path of convenience, which is closely allied to mechanical behavior.*

I want to write something that actually feels like I should say it, tell it. I want to write about Uncle Jason's long hair that my great-grandmother made him cut. I want to write about the drugs. I want to write about something his famous friend Sam Aaronson said, about the way he was always hobbling up the staircases of the music academy in Basel with the viola da gamba on his back.

I put pen to paper. Nothing comes out.

I'm looking through the window at a couple locking up their bikes outside in the rack by the red *Sacramento News & Review* stand. He wraps his arm around her shoulders, and she wraps hers around his waist. They walk through the door and stand at the bar, looking at the tiny menu.

"What do you want?" she seems to ask.

I put pen back to paper.

───────────

I want to ride bikes through the grid of this town with somebody, my hair long and blowing in the wind. I want to park our bikes in the rack and hold hands, walking down the street to fancy coffee.

I want our bodies to be made of all the same ingredients. I want to cook all of our meals together. I want to tell him about myself for hours at the kitchen table with a glass vase of sunflowers, and I never want to stop, except for when he tells me about himself. Then I want to listen forever. For the first time in my life, I want to listen as much as I want to talk.

I want him to touch my circular central line scar in broad daylight in a light blue bedroom. I want him to run his fingers over it, where my skin healed in a thin layer, a millimeter of skin separating my heart from the world. I want him to ask me what the scar is from, and I want to give him a real answer. I don't want to undermine it. I don't want to say that I'm better now. I want to tell him that I will always have cancer as a child. I want to tell him that cancer is the thing I am closest to in this world.

I want him to think my central line scar is strong, beautiful—no, I want him to think my central line scar is attractive—like Hollywood. I want what my body is capable of to turn somebody on.

I want him to take me to the movies on a Saturday night. I want him to put his arm around me during the St. Jude's commercial before the previews, and not say anything. I want to watch TV all day with him and get to a St. Jude's commercial and hear "Everyone knows someone affected by cancer, a friend, a family member, a teacher." I want to hear him turn to me and say, "And my sexy girlfriend," and I want to laugh, and I want him to laugh too. I want that to be the first time he calls me his girlfriend. I want him to come over to me and wrap himself around my healthy body.

I want somebody I can be new with. I want somebody who says yes when I ask him to marry me. I want it to be legal, written into the state of California, into the state of this country, that my body fell deep down into someone else's and doesn't want to get out. I want to be a new body with him; I want to be too close, to lose my sense of self in him. I want somebody I can be a *they* with. I want to lie in bed with our single body and for him to say, "Let's switch hearts." We close our eyes. "Let's switch tongues." I want to push it further, feeling no insecurity. "Let's mix our childhood blood." We close our eyes and regenerate it, but it's strange; our cells can still tell who we are. My *white* won't touch his *red*. We lie here in our childhood blood, bleeding into each other, and the words *switch back, unmix,* erase from our vocabulary, forever.

I want to make a new family so if I get cancer again, the family I grew up in can be the secondary family, the family whose role is just to help, the family who doesn't have to go through it. My new body gets pregnant easily, no complications from the chemo it had during puberty. The only problem is that I want the baby to stay with me. They have to slice me open to get her out. Then I am pregnant again, and so on. We have five kids, all cancer-less, running around the house. I whisper in their ears, "Please grow up quickly." I need them to take care of me, to help my husband, to learn the burden of my body in a family.

I tell the children that I'm sorry. I write a book about how sorry I am, begging forgiveness. *Realize this.* I want somebody to realize how selfish cancer has made me. I want somebody to realize how much I give to my friendships, how I have always kept close friends, how I call often, not only because I love them, but because it is my deepest animal instinct to build a tribe, to give and receive love, to surround myself with people who will write me letters when my body fails again.

Mel asks if I want to go out for drinks tonight, to happy hour. She's in town from Oakland, staying at her parents' house.

I wind down Land Park Drive to pick her up, past the leaves on the sidewalks and the old two-story houses. I park on the street of her parents' five-way intersection, looking through the fence to the yard where the rope swing used to be. I remember swinging there when I came home from the hospital. My pink wig flew off my head and into the grass.

When Mel opens the front door, I expect Tanner to run up to me, her old dog, the terrier. But it's Pearl now. She's cuter and smaller, with way more energy.

"Hi!" Mel says, with one side of her body leaning down, trying to control the jumping Pearl. Dr. Arnold walks up, and we all talk at the door.

————————

It's freezing at the bar, where they're playing some experimental film and anxiety-provoking band. This place isn't cool to me anymore; it just seems strange, or like it's trying too hard now that Sacramento's on the map. I want to go to a new bar, but it's too late. We order beers to bring outside and pay separately, which feels awkward and unnatural for us. I'm used to one of our parents giving us a twenty dollar bill to walk to get ice cream or sandwiches together as kids.

We go outside to get a table under the headlamps. Doug Appel, one of the most popular guys from my middle school, comes over to say hi.

"I've read your articles in the *Sac News & Review*, Maia," he says. "Cool that you moved back to Sac. I moved back too, a few months ago. I live with Jack. Remember him? Good times."

We make small talk until some hipster girl waves Doug back to her table.

"I can't believe Doug remembers me," I say to Mel. "But I did get cancer in seventh grade, so I guess that makes me pretty memorable."

"Maybe he remembers you because you were cool."

"I just have this idea that, because I wasn't attractive and had a buzz cut at Sutter, no one could see me or something."

I start telling her about Doug's roommate, my middle school lab partner.

"Well, I think he liked me. Actually, I know he did, but I wouldn't admit that to myself or anybody else. It made no sense that he would."

"Why?"

"Because who would like the sick girl? Once I was walking behind a group of guys, and they were teasing Jack for having a crush on me. He would joke around with me and stuff. They couldn't believe he could like someone who looked like me."

"Are you sure it had so much to do with you?"

"What do you mean?"

"Maybe they were just asshole middle school boys teasing their friend, another asshole middle school boy, for having a crush."

I'd never thought of that before.

"Maybe."

"And seriously, you may have been in recovery, but you still had boobs! Remember when you came back from the hospital, and a few months later, you got your central line removed? Remember I came over to swim?"

"Yeah, because I couldn't swim with the central line in."

"You put on your swimsuit, and it was insane. I mean, who grows boobs during cancer treatment?"

I laugh, but now I don't want to talk about cancer anymore. I feel like the people next to us are getting weirded out.

"Do you think you and Jay will get married? Do you guys ever talk about it?" I ask, changing the subject.

"Yeah, we talk about it all the time."

———————

Mel and I stand in her driveway and tell each other how much we mean to each other, how much we miss each other.

"I'm so excited you're visiting in a few weeks," she says. "I'm sorry it took so long for us to start hanging out again. I was so mean after your cancer, when we were kids."

"You were mean? I was mean! I was horrible to you."

"What were we even fighting about?"

"Making new friends, right? Sharing each other?"

"What the hell!"

"It seems dumb now, but it was so intense and real, heightened by everything we had gone through."

It stresses me out to talk about what happened with us, even in a surface level way like this. I don't want to go any deeper, to remember the horrible things we went through back then. I'm worried we couldn't actually start this friendship over if we do. I'm worried we'll just go back to Christmas and birthday text messages.

———————————

I drive back to my house. Jane's there again, passed out on the couch. She doesn't look good. There's no color in her cheeks. She's cuddled up in the rainbow blanket from the closet, the one she likes the best. The TV is on, playing the final credits of *Music and Lyrics.* She wakes up as I close the door.

"I know you just got home, but I need to vent. I'm so pissed at my roommate."

"What happened this time?" I ask, sitting down on the couch next to her.

"She's leaving her hat in the toilet again!"

Jane's talking about the plastic specimen collector that looks like an upside-down top hat. It goes under the toilet seat and collects urine and stool so the nurses can check on it later.

"She needs to move the hat to the ground when she's finished! It's not that hard!"

"That's so annoying," I say. "Chemo-pee is so gross, too, way grosser than regular pee."

"It's blue, Maia, literally. Not just green—*blue*. But that's not even the worst of it."

"Geez, what else does she do?"

"She'll leave number two in there! And if she does move it to the ground, she never covers it with a paper towel."

"Ew," I say, relating, remembering the experience exactly.

"I mean, for Pete's sake, it's just proper bathroom etiquette to move it to the ground and cover it up."

I can hear my neighbor playing faint acoustic guitar on his porch across the street. He plays a familiar tune now, bluesy, but I can't put my finger on it. I go to the window. The sky is pink and red behind him.

I want to go to him. I want to sit out and listen to him play guitar as the sun goes down and the trees turn black around us.

But I don't. I listen to Jane talk shit instead.

"And then, her machines will be beeping in the middle of the night, and she doesn't wake up! And neither does her mom! So *I* have to call the nurse for her!"

I get a vancomycin ball from the back of the refrigerator and a disinfectant wipe. I go over to Jane. I disinfect her central line tube, the blue spout this time. I attach the vancomycin ball and watch the antibiotic drain into her. I sit down next to Jane, and restart the movie.

CHAPTER 5

Hair Is Youthful

When I was twelve, I moved into the home office, declaring I should have my own space, taking the desk and printer out, hanging my door beads and posters on the walls. My parents pushed my twin bed over the Wi-Fi router, and my mom painted the white walls blue.

I got cancer a year later and never slept in that room again. No one does. No one even goes in there, except to pay bills, print, and leave. My attempt at independence, at a cool teenage room, is a home office again, a cancer-causing workspace.

When I go to my parents' house for Thanksgiving dinner, I share a room with Alex.

She snores next to me. I can't sleep. I try to write on my phone. I stare at a Google search of the Rhine, Basel—the river that murdered my uncle Jason Paras on July 14, 1982—and notice the streets, the trees, the couples, the stones, the sky, the sunset, the water, the blue-green water. In the pictures, cars float slowly over the cobblestone streets that surround it, and couples pass over the bridge. They stop and look out, smile, love each other.

Old memories race through me, some secondhand, some made-up. Most importantly, none of them are my own. I can write that

Uncle Jason is there on that bridge, walking with friends back from rehearsal, late at night with a lover, back from teaching at the Schola, the Music Academy of Basel. He has a viola da gamba on his back, an ache, a tune in his head, that good bit. Or he's back from the tour in Italy, stopping on the bridge's stone railing to write a short letter to Del Dayo Drive, Sacramento, California. He creates an identity, a voice for himself when he's gone. He writes it for his only intrigued niece to find and use in his biography, thirty-five years later.

Here on Google Images, there are little boats and geese and a bridge, and my uncle Jason who couldn't breathe. My uncle inhaled a throat full of water and didn't even wave his arms or cry out. He just drowned. And moved through the current of the "Blue in Green," like Miles Davis says, or plays, or feels. What if my uncle's body was breathing, alive and well, present at every Thanksgiving dinner, with his "better than my mom" baroque musician attitude? What if one year, when I was still a teenager, he looked across the table and saw a tiny artsy side in me? He'd start bossing me around, telling me what I should listen to. He would've made me stick with jazz instead of trying to become a writer, so I'd never have to explain anything, and I could just feel it. He'd pass me a note under the table: *You can't hurt your sisters' feelings in a saxophone solo.*

Today at Thanksgiving dinner, Elaine said I talk about myself too much. Slicing the turkey, my dad joked back, "You talk about yourself, and then you go and write about yourself." I laugh at this; everybody laughs at this. It's funny. But now I sit awake at night, wanting to be normal again. I want to get another job in customer service doing the thing I'm best at—fake smiling. I think I'll burn the *Little Heart Book,* Uncle Jason's biography, the diaries. Everything I've ever hoarded. I'm embarrassed by it all—or no, I'm just ashamed. As much as I love my family, something about being all together like this makes me feel like I'm *trying* to be who I am, like my whole life is an attempt. I went through something strange as a kid, and now I'm just trying to figure out how to live, how to be normal, still, eleven years later. I never wanted to drink coffee so strong, live alone, talk to myself about myself. All I ever wanted was to tell somebody something about a thirteen-year-old girl with a different name.

———

"Hair is youthful," my mom says the next morning, as she cracks eggs into a hot pan. My sisters and I sit on the kitchen floor, the office just down the hall. We lie around in sweatpants and big pajama T-shirts, petting the cats. We all look like teenagers again—Elaine out of her business casual, Alex out of her internship scrubs.

"The butt strip is the best," I say.

"Yeah. That part doesn't hurt at all," says Alex.

"Do you guys take it all off?" I ask.

"I don't get why people don't. That's the point. That's what you're paying for," says Elaine, holding Lady Bird up in the air. The kitten meows. She wants to be set back down.

"Just remember, eventually it won't grow back," my mom says, flipping the eggs. "And you might want some hair there someday."

Honeyboy jumps out of my lap. He's my favorite of the cats, the oldest.

"I actually haven't waxed in a year," I say.

"You shave?" asks Alex.

"I don't know, just maintenance."

"That's so gross, Maia," says Elaine. "We're Greek. I mean, seriously, it's like, thick. We'll go today."

She looks something up on her humongous iPhone and makes a call.

———

I lie flat on my back on the waxing table. The room is like a doctor's office or procedure room, but there's a poster on the wall of a woman with skinny shiny legs. She's hairless, except on her head, thick, curly brown locks. She struts down a cobblestone street in a red dress with a slogan floating at her right: *walk in, strut out.* I silently joke to myself; instead of that poster, there's a big sign in the red frame: *Warning: Lying on this vagina waxing table and submitting to great pain may remind you of your collapsing lung catastrophe eleven years ago.*

"Butterfly your legs," my waxer, Katie, tells me. She spreads purple wax all over one side of me and waits a few seconds for it to harden.

"Did you have a nice Thanksgiving?"

"Yeah, I just had dinner with my family. My sisters are home from LA."

Rip.

It's terrible but feels somehow productive. I take a deep breath.

"You okay?"

"Yeah. It's just been a while since I've been here, clearly. Will you leave a little hair at the top?"

"A landing strip?"

"Uh, no. Could you make it look kind of natural?"

She's done in seven rips and a few plucks and asks me to look in the mirror, to see if my vagina is how I'd like it.

It looks like my bald head when I was in the hospital, smooth, soft, with a little bit of hair left. It's like when I was in my second round of chemo. Not all of my hair cells were dead yet. Some still grew, hung on in patches.

I go to the counter to pay, rejecting the slow-growth serums they try to get me to buy. I schedule an appointment for next month that I know I'll forget about. Before I leave, I walk back down the hall to the bathroom.

I accidentally open the door on somebody.

"*Shit, fuck,* I'm so sorry—wait, what?"

"It's fine, Maia, come in," says Jane, sitting there on the toilet with her corduroy pants down, her green-striped underwear between her knees. "You should really stop cursing so much. It's so negative."

I lock the door and lean against it.

"What are you doing here, Jane?"

"Why would you do that to yourself, let them rip out your hair like that? And on your privates! You're crazy. Hair is youthful," she says, starting to pee. She leans her elbows on her knees and holds her chin in her hands.

"Because I'm a hairy Greek woman? It feels really clean and nice, too."

"Hair doesn't make you dirty, Maia."

"I just thought maybe it would make me feel more confident."

"You mean, because of . . . sex?"

"Well, yeah, I guess so."

"I thought you didn't even like that anyways. Remember with Tim?"

"I'm not as insecure about my body anymore," I say, not sure if it's completely true.

"If you're gonna do it, you need to do it with a survivor. Cancer survivors date other cancer survivors, like in the movies."

"You should get that dating app," I say, teasing her.

"I won't need it. I'll meet someone naturally, through volunteer work at the hospital." Jane says. "He'll love me so much he won't care what's going on down there."

She looks down. "Geez, I barely even have pubes anymore. After the first round of chemo, it started falling out like this." She shows me her underwear, covered in tiny dead hairs. "I hated it when it started growing, but now I kinda miss it. Is that normal?"

She gets off the toilet and I see she's peed in a plastic "hat." She moves it slowly and steadily to the ground. I feel myself engage my core, remembering the way it made the move easier, less prone to a spill. Jane succeeds, sets the container of urine on the ground so the nurse can test it later. She washes her hands three times with hot water and fixes her pink wig's bangs in the mirror.

———————————

Elaine is waiting for me out in the car. Her Jetta is new and clean, slick, nothing like the car we used to share in high school. I look around for something, anything to remind me of our childhood selves, when we were young and close, driving to soccer practice on the same team. I'm looking for an empty water bottle, a Subway bag, a sweatshirt, extra soccer shorts or high socks, a beat-up SAT prep book, but there's nothing. There are only sunglasses in the cupholder.

"Mom just called and screamed at me because I fed the dogs the wrong food," she says, starting the car. "I mean, what the fuck? They're not my dogs! I'm not a kid anymore. She can't yell at me like that. And why does she get so angry?"

"Maybe that's exactly why she's mad, because you don't know how to feed them. Maybe she wants you to come home enough that you would know the new ways."

"This is why I don't live here anymore. I hate coming home."

"I don't really get why."

"I just hate it. I don't have good memories here. High school was horrible for me."

A car merges in front of us. Its vanity plate says *EZVIBES*.

"I think it's really nice, being with Mom and Dad."

"Your time in that house was different than mine. There's a lot you weren't there for."

"You mean when I was sick?"

"I don't even want to get into it. But Mom and Dad were different. Mom and I fought, and I'd just started high school."

"I know. I'm sorry."

The trees on either side of the street sway back and forth as the wind picks up.

"That's not what I meant. It's not your fault, Maia."

"I know," I say, reminding myself.

She turns on the radio and scrolls to 107.9 The End, the pop station we used to listen to on the way to school. But it's only static. It doesn't exist anymore. She turns the radio off.

"Okay, let's stop talking about this. How was the wax?"

"It was good. Didn't you see me *strut out*?"

We laugh a bit, but not enough. It's still sad in the car as she turns onto Watt Avenue.

———————————

Later, we go to the Arden Fall Mall to see *A Star Is Born* with my mom and Alex. We take Alta Arden instead of Arden Way like we always do, to avoid traffic, and turn off of Ethan by the In-N-Out Burger, heading to the back lot.

My mom parks and leans back to get her huge purse from behind her seat. She brought snacks for us, just like when we were kids.

"There's Boom Chicka Pop and La Croix, apple slices, and nuts," she says. "Also, I pre-bought tickets, so we can just walk right to the front."

She passes the printed papers out to us.

"Thanks, but I'm not eating that stuff," says Alex. "You don't need to pack us healthy snacks anymore."

"I'm just trying to make it fun."

"Give me a break," Alex mumbles, getting out of the car.

We start walking toward the theater.

"We go over and over this, but when will it end? When will you realize how much I do for you?" says my mom.

"We're adults," Alex snaps back. "You don't need to keep micromanaging our health."

"I never micromanaged. I just wanted to keep you as healthy as possible. I've let this all go, managing the lives of all of you girls."

Alex stops walking. She glares at the back of Mom's head.

"Oh, so now you don't care? You ruined my life for years with your goddamn shiitake fucking mushrooms, and now you say you don't care?"

Elaine and I are silent, giving each other crazy-eyed looks, praying together that this will end.

"I'm getting a drink. I'm getting a diet fucking soda."

"That's enough! I can't take this!" my mom wails through the parking lot.

She storms back to the car. Her body doesn't look like her body anymore; she looks like somebody else. It's her shoulders, moving through the world in fury, like a magnet flying toward the truck.

My sisters and I don't know what to do. We just stand there, until I finally say, "Alex, are you serious? If you're so adult, then why don't you grow up? Go tell her you're sorry."

From inside the theater, Elaine and I look through the glass wall at Alex and my mom in the parking lot yelling at each other 200 feet away. We can't understand anything they say, but we know it's a combination of the same sentences over and over again, the same sentences that echoed through our house for years and years growing up.

"I'm going back out there," I tell Elaine.

"Why?"

"Because we're supposed to be having a nice time."

"There's nothing you can say to make it better, Maia. They're not going to change," Elaine says. "You just always have to be the perfect kid, the favorite."

She turns around and walks toward the bathroom.

What she says hurts, but she's not wrong. I am a suck-up to my parents. I can't stand it when my mom is upset. I have an unhealthy need for her to be okay. I walk through the glass doors, thinking of what to say to make them stop yelling at each other, but Elaine's right. I have nothing. I stand on the sidewalk and listen.

"Not everything has to do with you! There are other things, other fucking things in the world other than you! It was rude what you said. It was just rude!" says my mom.

Somehow, they settle it, like they always do, though it's never resolved.

"Someone should've helped him more," says Elaine on the car ride home. She's talking about the main character in the movie.

"In a tweet, Ariana Grande said that it wasn't her responsibility to help Mac Miller, that she wasn't supposed to be somebody's caretaker," I say.

"That's just heartless."

"Yeah, it's your duty as a girlfriend to help," says Alex.

"I mean, you can't just, like, force somebody into rehab," I say. "They have to choose it. People have to ask for help."

We feel the topic leading into a fight, so we let it fade out. We sit quietly for a few moments as we pass Arden Middle on our right, where my parents went to school.

"The schools here suck," says Elaine.

"What are you talking about?" I ask. "The schools here are great. People from San Francisco are moving for them."

"That's just because they can't afford the Bay."

She's right, but I don't want to admit it. When she hates on Sacramento, it makes me insecure about my choice to move back here, like I'm some kind of failure.

"You're just wrong," I tell her.

"Elaine, Maia, relax," says Mom. "But yeah, I think the schools here are decent."

"So, Maia, what's your new guy's name?" asks Alex.

"I don't have a new guy."

"Elaine told me you like somebody in your neighborhood."

"He anything like Dean in New York with the greasy hair?" says Elaine. "You sure know how to pick em, Maia."

I come back hard.

"How are those Tinder dates? Meet anyone cool lately, any models with good ab photos prepping to ghost you?"

"Stop it. Just stop it!" my mom raises her voice.

"Mom, I was kidding."

"No, you weren't. You girls are horrible to each other! Don't you see it?"

We all go silent.

"Wow. It's gotten so bad that you just think it's normal now, the sass."

"We're having a nice time, Mom."

"A nice time? You're constantly arguing with each other, one-upping each other, making fun of each other's lifestyles. You think this is a nice time?"

"You're just mad at me from earlier," says Alex. "Don't take it out on all of us."

"We're just being sisters," I say.

"This isn't how sisters should be. You girls are horrible to each other, horrible to me."

"Why are you freaking out? We're sorry, Mom."

"You girls don't even know. Someday you'll be old. You'll be old, and then you'll be dead. You will look back, and you will have missed your chance to be close, to be there for each other."

You girls. The girls. The daughters. The times I've felt closest to my sisters in the last few years is when my mom is yelling at us like this, making us a collective. In my mother's anger, we become one body.

This might explain Jane.

I think I wanted somebody, a sister, who had the exact same body, a body who went through the exact same thing, at the exact same age. A sister just like me.

I found her one day when I was Googling the Rhine, looking for my uncle. On Google Images, there was a castle and a boat and an orange sky, the blue-green lingering beneath it, and then I was there. I walked along a cobblestone path and passed a group of people, all tanning. A woman with long dark hair leaning back on her palms smiled at me, one of my uncle's ex-girlfriends I supposed. She looked back toward the Rhine, desire in her eyes, looking out on the blue green. Each memory, each tragedy, became a small Rhine on its own, drifting through my body, through my arms and average heart. I wanted to talk to her, the girlfriend, the stranger, but I didn't.

Something told me to walk on. I felt it—poems, a complicated past, youth, something that knew what I desired. A hand came out of the blue green. I ran and jumped in, swimming farther and farther out. I heard the crash of my uncle's girlfriend coming in after me. My blood was seeping through my skin behind me, turning the blue green into red as I swam in perfect form. I took my uncle Jason's hand, his body too heavy, his body having composed itself into the water. I looked to his girlfriend in the blue green now too, and back to the eyes of Uncle Jason, alive, smiling at me through the water, slipping, and knew we would never speak. The girlfriend was drowning and pointing to my left, to a hand reaching in, fifteen feet away. A young hand, a hand of a child. I swam to it, as fast as I could, held on to it. A message spoke through our skin and hands; she was finally here, born again—a *me* but different. She pulled me up, and we flew together back home to Sacramento, California, where Neon Jane promised she would never let me go.

CHAPTER 6
Photograph

I don't feel it in my body. I don't feel the heaviness. I don't feel the cells. I feel like I do on a regular day. I feel just like me. But last Monday something was wrong; I felt an abnormal tiredness, a frustration in getting out of bed. A discombobulation inside me. So I went to get my blood tested.

I swear, I am a responsible cancer survivor. I eat well (organic), use turmeric, essential oils, avoid excessive red meat, dairy. I live as stress-free as one can. I meditate. I exercise. I put my body first. But this morning, I woke to a doctor's call, and that was it. "We need you to come in today, to talk in person. I'll meet you right outside the hospital." Now I'm thirteen again, standing in the hospital parking lot with my mother and my pediatrician. He says I have to walk forward. He says I have to walk through the automatic doors.

Once I know it's inside me, then it exists. But I can still rise out of bed. I drag myself through the house, cancer becoming me now. It feels warm throughout me, then ice cold. Occasionally it bites. In the kitchen, the wooden angel drowns in a clogged sink of soaking dishes. God, I hate her—what a drama queen, look at her, drowning herself! I tell her she has to get out, get up, start breathing again. I place her back on the shelf, and there she stands, arms up, soaking wet, feeling nothing at all.

I slide my body down the counter to the ground, lean back against the cabinet sitting on the floor, legs straight out. I let leukemia float around inside me, a ghost in my blood. It's not as mean as you'd think; it just has a problem. It whispers to me, saying, "I'm sorry." The ghost is just a series of mistakes, a cancerholic living inside me, thriving off the recreation of its cells. The cancerholic sits on a brown couch in my gut, drinking beers filled with cancer. Endless empties surround. The cancerholic apologizes again, belligerent, makes more of itself. But it doesn't mean it. It just can't stop. The little addict in me has relapsed again, stabbed me in the back, feels terrible for it. Back to rehab. It's sorry. It's sorry it was born in the first place. Sometimes it wishes it had never been born at all.

Am I too infested already to go see the movie *Bohemian Rhapsody* before I go into the hospital indefinitely, or into one hospital and get transferred by ambulance to another one that's fancier, better? I think I want music to teach me how to write, and my uncle's album is boring to me. Slow, sad, dreary baroque? I want rock and roll, a beat, gospel, something unheard of. I want to write with an electric guitar. I want to write with a chorus behind me, with backup singers behind every word. I don't want to say these things alone. Say my words with me, belt them like you feel them too, like you're a survivor and I've said something you've felt for your entire life. Haven't I? If you don't want to sing what I sing, then please just dance with me. Don't leave me on the floor here all alone.

I don't want Jane to see me. I'm so embarrassed. But my leukemia's back, and she has to know, or does she already? Her wheels grow louder and louder against the sidewalk outside, moving closer to my front door. Now I can't breathe. My heart races—tachycardia, or just relapse, nerves. Jane first, then I'll call my mom, tell her to meet me in the parking lot of the hospital where they tried to kill me before.

———————

I wake up sweating in my orange bed. Lying here on my back,

facing the white ceiling, I know there aren't cancer cells inside of me. It was only a dream.

I read something once, that there is cancer inside all of us. Apparently our cells are malfunctioning all the time, eating each other, screwing up, but it's only when it happens in large capacities that it's noticed, that it harms us. I believe this is what happens in my nightmares. Cancer has begun again inside of me, but my body is able to conquer it this time. As I wake, it knows to leave me alone.

When I was actually sick, I never felt the cancer cells in my body. I only felt cancer through other parts of me—my head, my skin, my energy level. It made other parts of me show me its existence.

In my desk drawer, I have one secret photo of myself when I was sick, but I try not to bring it out. I don't want it to screw with the aura of the house, my safe space, or scare Jane. It's in an envelope at the far back, under some sketchbooks from college. In the photo, I have no eyebrows, no eyelashes. I have no color in my face. I wear a green T-shirt, a gray zip-up sweatshirt with stars on it, and a necklace with a starfish charm, high neck, choker-like. Strands of my neon pink wig are out of place, messy. There's a blue clip-on bow on its left side. I'm sick in the photo, but I'm not unrecognizable—though I don't think I look anything like Neon Jane. I look like a real person, like myself. I look real—like a kid.

Tonight, Mel and I are looking at a box of photos and letters she kept from childhood. She finds a picture of us when I was sick. We have our arms around each other, smiling. I'm wearing the neon pink wig. She has hair to her ears, pulled back in a grey athletic headband. She donated her hair that year. I remember taking this picture toward the end of my treatment when she came to visit me. I remember taking it off my bulletin board when my high school boyfriend came over for the first time and we hung out in my room, keeping the door wide open.

Mel looks through the box and pulls out a handmade card. I recognize my scrawny handwriting immediately. *Happy Birthday, Mel Bell!* it says on the cover, with a drawing of a cake. She passes it to me.

I love you sooo much. You are the greatest friend a leukemia fighter could have! I am so lucky 2 have a friend like you. I'm your stalker! Love, Maia. P.S. Guess what? Chicken butt! P.S.S. Where's my nurse?

"Where's my nurse!" I read out loud, laughing, remembering the inside joke we'd say when we wanted someone to bring us something and were feeling lazy. I pass the card back to Mel. She laughs at it too.

I sit down in her desk chair and crisscross my legs.

"Ugh, all this stuff is so crazy to look at. I just feel so different from that person, but the same. I don't really know how to explain it," I say.

"I feel that way too about that whole time period. I don't really remember anything about seventh grade actually, except for you being sick, and visiting you."

I can't imagine what it must've been like for Mel to watch her best friend deteriorate and come back to life again. I called her every night during cancer. Bone marrow aspirations, transfusions, allergic reactions—I told her everything that was going on, and everything I felt about it. I had no filter.

I wonder what Mel's family talked about after she hung up with me, or after a weekend visit to see me in the hospital. I wonder if it was ever too much for her. Was there a discussion between her parents when I was first diagnosed, about how much they would allow my illness to be a shared trauma? She wasn't like my sisters; she didn't have to see it. She had a choice.

"Sometimes cancer seems harder now than it was before, if that makes sense," I say.

"What do you mean?"

"Just being sick and processing being sick."

"I think about that a lot too, how specific of an experience that was. Sometimes it just seems like this normal part of my childhood, that you were sick, and I went to visit you, like everyone had a friend suffering from a disease in childhood."

Mel picks Pearl up from the floor and puts her on the bed. I go over to pet her.

"I feel like people forget it happened, like my family. I feel like everybody processed it and moved on. I'm still just stuck in the past."

"No one's going to forget what you went through."

"But maybe they should! Maybe we should all just be done with this. I mean, it's over, isn't it?"

"I guess."

"I think my sisters are annoyed that my parents are giving me money right now and that I'm trying to write. Elaine said they would never do this for her. But this cancer thing is taking over my life. I can't be happy unless I'm processing cancer, which in turn makes me sad. It's so twisted. Ugh, I'm sorry. I'm really sorry for dumping this on you."

"It's fine, seriously."

I want to explain things to Mel, how bad things really are. I'm surprised by how easy it is for me to talk about cancer with her again. I lie down on the bed and face the ceiling.

"Sometimes I feel like my previous self, myself as a kid, is haunting me, like she won't leave me alone. She doesn't think I'm successful enough or a good enough cancer survivor."

"I feel like that too, though, in my own way."

"You do?"

"I'm not totally the person I thought I'd be when I was younger."

"You're closer to being her than I am."

Driving home, Jane sits in the passenger seat with her feet up on my dashboard, leaning back lazily with her arms crossed.

"You should stop dumping on her like that," says Jane.

"Who?"

"Your friend! You're going to tire her out. She can only handle so much. Maybe that's why things went wrong with your friendship before."

I don't say anything. Jane goes on.

"You need to stop, you know, talking about all your feelings all the time. Mel already did enough, helped you during cancer, talked to you. She's only one person."

"So you think that when your cancer ends, you're not going to need to talk to anyone about it? I mean, actually, do you even talk about it now?"

"I have my journal. And I have a best friend too. But I'm going to stop talking about cancer with her when I get better. Then we'll be best friends forever."

"That's enough for you? Talking about cancer during treatment only, and then pretending it never happened, but still wanting to be an oncologist when you grow up? It's enough for you to talk to a journal who doesn't say anything back?"

Jane sits up and looks out the car window.

"I don't need anyone to say anything back. I don't need to have those negative feelings in the journal said out loud. Negative feelings about the cancer experience should just be released, and then let go, into nothingness."

"Oh, and I'm the cancer hippie."

Jane rolls her eyes at me.

"All I'm saying is that you're gonna lose her as a friend again if you keep dumping on her. No one wants to talk about cancer forever and ever."

"I don't think that's how Mel feels though."

"Well, it's how she should feel, if she's a normal person! I mean it's just going on for too long, Maia! Your cancer wasn't even that bad. What was it, a year? Less than a year? Other kids have it for two, three, four years, some even longer! If she doesn't feel over it by now, she'll feel it sooner or later. You have to stop talking about it, not just to her, but to everyone."

I roll the windows down, take a deep breath of fresh air.

"What if I can't?"

"You can."

"What if this is the only thing I'll be able to talk about, earnestly, for the rest of my life."

"Then that is kind of pathetic."

I pull over in front of a CVS Pharmacy.

"If you're going to make me feel bad about myself for the whole drive, you can walk home."

We sit in silence for a moment.

"I'm sorry, okay?" Jane finally says. "I'm just annoyed. I think it's wrong what you're doing, letting your experience define your whole life, your friendships. I just want to go home. Just take us home," she says.

I don't buy it.

"What's going on with you?"

She stares blankly forward at a man carrying a bag of groceries across the street and a bunch of yoga girls walking behind him. She looks back at me.

"They think I have to have a bone marrow transplant, okay? The chemo isn't working like they thought. I had the MRD test. There are still cells left."

"But you're only in your third round of chemo. Of course there are still cells."

"Well, they're concerned. They're looking for a bone marrow match for me."

"Jane, come on, I don't think you'll need that."

"Oh, well, if you say everything's okay, then I guess it is! Because you know everything! You're so much smarter than me! Hey, why don't I just get some turmeric essential oil instead to cure this thing inside of me? Or how about this? How about I just meditate my cancer cells away?! Just drop me off at yoga. It's right around the corner."

"I'm trying to help you. I'm always trying to help you."

"People die from the transplant, Maia."

Suddenly, Jane starts to cry. She throws the pink wig on the dashboard and scratches her itchy, bald head. She puts her sweatshirt hood up.

"I don't want to be like all the kids with the transplants. I don't want to wear that mask. I don't want to look like that, like a robot. I don't want to swell up from steroids. I don't want to live in the ICU. I don't think my body can handle it anyways, someone else's blood cells."

Jane is too weak to sob, so she just cries, tears streaming down her face. She closes her eyes, leans her head into my chest, wipes her tears on her sleeve.

———————

I stop at the grocery store to get more turmeric. Maybe I'll buy some for Jane, just as a joke to cheer her up. She says she doesn't want to get out of the car. She says she's too tired after crying so hard.

I'm standing in the checkout line when I hear somebody say my name.

"Hey, Maia!"

To my right, I see Cassie Jones, a girl who went to my elementary school. She's an Instagram famous health blogger now, blogging all about healthy food and lifestyle. She was recently diagnosed with Lyme's Disease. She posts about that a lot, showing different ways she cares for herself, different all-natural treatments she uses.

Sometimes I look at Cassie's Instagram and think that I could've been her, or somebody like her. I could've been the girl from Sacramento who got famous from health-oriented writing. I could've taken cancer and run with it. But I never did. I was always too afraid of it.

We make small talk for a minute.

"It's so good to see you. I was just in Manhattan and thought of you. I wondered if you were still living out there," Cassie says.

"Oh, yeah, I graduated a few years ago and moved back here. It's better for me, I think. I was pretty overwhelmed out there."

"I think California has been better for me too."

A man walks up next to her, shows her a brand of protein powder.

"Dad, this is Maia. She went to school with me."

"Nice to meet you," he says as we shake hands. "Oh," he says again, "are you Maia, the orthodontist's daughter who was sick?"

"Yeah, that's me," I say.

"Wow, you look great."

"Thanks."

I give Cassie a hug and tell her it's nice to see her. She walks with her dad back through the store. I step in line to buy the turmeric.

The woman checking out in front of me turns around.

"You're the girl who got leukemia in 2007?"

I nod, embarrassed. She stares at me for a moment, the expression changing on her face.

"I'm so sorry that happened to you, honey. I'm a friend of your mom's from high school. She was so torn up about it."

"Oh, thanks. I actually forgot to get something. It was nice talking to you."

I walk back down the coffee aisle, past the tea, the chocolate. I head to the bread, or to anywhere I can have a moment.

"The orthodontist's daughter?"

A woman pushing a toddler in her cart is coming toward me. The toddler starts crying.

"Wow, you look amazing! What a miracle! And your dad did such a great job on my teeth!" she smiles. "Invisalign, it's *reaaally* something!"

"Oh, hi, I, uh, I have to go," I turn around, heading toward the pastas and sauce.

"Was it just terrible, *koukla*? To have cancer?"

A Greek lady from the orthodox church is standing in the middle of the aisle, with a cart full of steaks.

"What was it like, honey? What did it feel like? Baklava?"

She reaches her hand out to me, with one in her palm.

"John's daughter?" says somebody else, a man in a Fitness Rangers sweatshirt.

It never ends.

"Katherine's daughter?"

"The middle child!"

"The sick one!"

Voices from the whole store are coming toward me now, as I'm cornered by the raw meat and start to shrink, shrink, shrink, and turn into a little tiny New York strip, sitting in the glass window.

"Excuse me, ma'am, you're holding up the line."

I snap out of it, all of it.

"Ma'am, are you okay? How would you like to pay?"

"Oh, sorry. Cash."

CHAPTER 7

Tachycardia

My mom says she never fainted when I had my chest tube insertion after the central line surgery. She says she never left me alone. She says she was lying with her arms and head down on the table next to me, right next to me as I had the procedure, and then she couldn't move herself. She couldn't get up. The stress of it, the horror of it, paralyzed her body. She says she was there for it all, that she would never have left me alone during that. But I swear, the way I remember it, they took my mother away that day.

My memory about cancer is often inaccurate. I have a lot of things backwards. It's like I lived a different cancer than my mom. Sometimes, talking to her, everything I remember, feel, and believe about what happened to me turns out to be wrong, and I want to get it right. What was the anesthesiologists name again? What was the funny thing the paramedic said? How long did it take for the vancomycin to drain? I want the truth to survive, but in my childhood head, I wrote a cancer story, my chemo-brain playing tricks to find a beginning, middle, end. I was too drugged out to get everything right.

Jane hasn't come home for days, but I think of her often. I try to lean into this time without her, this time of focus. I apply to some jobs in offices, jobs I would never actually want to do. Then I get the fire back in my project about Uncle Jason. I pour myself into my work. Every morning, I sift through endless photos, letters, journals. I spread what's left of his life over my living room floor, looking for patterns, connections. Looking for something to say. I call his old friends, bandmates. I add Europeans on Facebook with long, detailed messages of who I am and what I'm trying to do. From these people, I figure out the person Jason was, and the person he could've been.

During his last year of life, Uncle Jason developed some kind of back pain. He had back spasms walking around the Schola campus. He'd have to lie flat on the ground and wait for his pain to go away. Most people think this is what killed my uncle that day in the Rhine. They think he had a back spasm out there in the water.

But I don't get it. Why would someone with chronic back pain go for a swim, especially somewhere with a heavy current? I'll never say it to anybody else, but sometimes I think my uncle was reckless with his life.

People say he was developing immense stress due to music. They say he put so much pressure on himself, that his back spasms were increasing in pain every day. Sue Salinger, who claims she was just a friend of Jason's, tells me she was out walking with him along the Rhine just a few months before, and he said some existential things, but she won't tell me exactly what he said.

It's like everyone is still protecting him. My uncle's dead body is guarded by an army of nerdy baroque musicians. And none of them will back down.

———————

Jane's sitting on the couch watching *Music and Lyrics*, her IV pole right next to her. She's at the scene where Hugh Grant and Drew Barrymore wake up under the piano.

I throw my bag on the chair next to us and sit down with her. She pauses the movie.

"How was writing?" she asks me.

"It was nice. I made some progress."

"Cool."

I can tell she's tired by her short response. She's pale, probably needing a blood transfusion. She stares off past me now, almost through me.

"You okay?"

"Yeah. I just need to talk to you about something. It's been a rough couple of days."

"Okay, tell me."

"I'm getting the bone marrow transplant for sure. They found somebody for me."

It doesn't make any sense. Jane and I are synced, and I never had the bone marrow transplant. I responded to chemotherapy. I stopped making cancer cells.

"What do you mean?"

"That's exactly what I mean! They're going to give me someone else's bone marrow. They're going to put me in the ICU."

"That doesn't make any sense."

She pauses.

"Why do you keep being like this?"

"Being like what?"

"Being so weak!" she stands up for a dramatic moment but quickly sits back down, feeling too tired. "It's almost like you don't think I'll get through it."

"Of course I think you'll get through it."

"Do you actually though?"

"Yes, Jane. I do," I say. I hug her. She won't hug me back.

"You don't have to treat me like I'm so much younger than you, like I'm some little kid."

"But you are a kid."

"Not anymore."

"It's going to be okay. You don't have to be scared."

"I'm not scared, Maia. I'm not."

"I never said you were. But it's also okay if you are. You're going through so much."

"That's enough!" she says, pushing my body away with the weakest bit of strength. "This is more uncomfortable than a cytarabine rash."

We sit silently for a moment.

"Why do we keep fighting? It's like . . . every time we talk now. We used to be so close. We used to be best friends."

I don't know how to respond.

———————

She passes out in my bed with the IV pole next to her, the tube coming out from the orange comforter. I stay up late working on Uncle Jason's biography at the kitchen table, trying to distract myself from the sadness and confusion of our previous conversation.

I'm trying to get an article out of a glass frame that hung in my grandmother's house. My mom gave it to me, thinking it might help with my project. It's a review of one of my uncle's records, "17th Century Music for Viola Da Gamba and Lyra Viol." I want to scan the article tomorrow, get a file of it on my computer, but it's hard to get out of the frame. There are so many screws and pieces. I keep trying to pry it open. Eventually I succeed.

I place the frame's glass and the rest of its pieces on the chair next to me and read through the article again. *Jason Paras was twenty-nine when he drowned while swimming in the Rhine in Switzerland last summer. This recording of a concert he gave six months before at Indiana University, where he was due to take up a position as a performer and teacher last fall, hints at what was lost by his death. Not only a specialist in early instruments, but a performer of world class . . .*

I look at Jason's face in the photo next to these words, his brown hair, dark beard, serious eyes. My uncle looks like Jesus Christ.

I think about what I've speculated before, that maybe my uncle Jason didn't want to live a long life. That maybe by twenty-nine, he was done with all of this. I think about something his ex-girlfriend, Marie Esposito, said in an interview, that Jason lived the kind of life the universe doesn't respond well to. She said that he wanted too much control over things. She said the world takes those who fight too hard against it.

I'm making up the life of a man from a time period I never lived in. I wonder about Jason's secrets, the things the baroque knows, what's written into his music, his scores. If my uncle Jason was depressed, then why? Depression doesn't have to be rooted in anything, doesn't really need a reason. But if there was one, then what was it? Fear? Fear of failure? Fear of his choices? Fear of himself?

I stand up and immediately feel something jab into me—a breaking, something inhuman, a slicing—in my right leg.

I feel the blood before I see it. I don't want to look down. The glass frame was chipped on one corner, sticking out from the chair next to me.

I force myself to look at it. My knee is split open, deep. It's bleeding more, spilling onto the carpet.

"Fuck, fuck!" I yell, hobbling to the kitchen, ripping off paper towels.

Jane walks in wearing her pink button-down pajama set. The vancomycin ball is in her shirt pocket, draining into her central line. She rubs her eyes with one hand and rolls her IV pole in the other.

"Maia? What happened? Are you okay?"

I start to laugh, feeling sort of out of it, woozy.

"Guess he wants the power of his own story back! Dammit, what am I going to write now? My own?"

"Maia, what are you talking about? Why are you laughing? This isn't funny! You're really hurt! Your cut is so deep. You can see white."

"It's funny, Jane. It's hilarious. My whole life is hilarious."

"You've got to go get stitched up."

"It's fine."

"You've got to go to the ER."

"You always ruin all the fun, Jane."

There's blood all over my hands now, from soaking it up with the towels. I awkwardly put on my jacket with my hand still over my knee.

────────────

At the urgent care center, I sit in the waiting room and fill out the paperwork, reading the questions.

Previous health concerns/surgery?

I check *No.*

An older lady sits down next to me. Her son, in a red Gap sweatshirt, looks like he's about to throw up.

"Oh my, look at that," she says, staring down at the blood seeping through my shitty bandage.

"Have you had stitches before?" the little boy asks me in his frail kid voice.

I don't know how to answer the question. Technically yes, but never like this.

"No."

"The medicine they use to numb the cut hurts a lot!" he says, educating me. "I had it when I crashed my bike and split my lip open last year."

Fell on your bike, kid? Please. I want to tell him that after everything I've been through, this kind of stuff is nothing to me.

But when they call me back and the doctor puts a huge needle straight into my wound, I want to cry. I want to scream out in pain. The kid was right, it does hurt, it hurts so much. No matter how much physical pain I've been in in the past, it still fucking hurts to get numbed for stitches from some stupid at-home accident. I'm twenty-four years old. No one stands next to me anymore. No one holds my hand. The second to last shot is the worst, but after that, I can't feel a thing. It feels like my knee doesn't belong to my body anymore, like the doctor is stitching up somebody else's knee, a knee I have no connection to, not even emotionally.

On the way back home, I call my mom. She says she wants to stop by, make sure I'm okay. She was already in midtown at dinner with a few friends.

She gets to the house before me, waiting in her car on the curb. I pull into the driveway, and we walk up to my front door together.

"Thanks for coming over. I'm totally fine, really," I say, turning my key in the lock.

"Well, I just wanted to say hi anyway."

I hear Jane's IV pole wheels rolling in the house, and then they abruptly stop.

"Wait, did you hear that?" My mom pulls me back. "Is there someone in here?"

"Mom, come on, relax. It's just us."

"No, I saw a shape or shadow or something in your room. Wait here."

She grabs an umbrella by the front door and slowly walks to the room. I try to stay calm, praying that Jane's figured out that my mom can still see her, even if it's just her outline.

"Mom, stop. Seriously, it's fine."

I hear her open my closet door and rustle things around a bit.

"Weird," she says, walking back toward me. "I don't know what I saw. Also, you need to clean your closet."

"I know."

She sits on the couch to relax. I get her a glass of water.

"You were watching *Music and Lyrics*?" she says, pointing to the paused TV. "I remember watching that together, when we had your blood transfusions in the day hospital."

"Yeah. It was our routine."

"How is the biography? Any job applications going out?"

"Yeah, a few. And I'm working on the one for the school's opening next semester, to teach writing."

"I know you'll figure it out. I think this is good for you, to take a bit of a break. You put so much pressure on yourself."

"I know," I say.

"How are you feeling about your heart?"

"Good."

"You still taking fish oil?"

"Yeah."

"I'm going to order you some CoQ10."

———————

When my mom leaves, I search the house for Jane. I find her standing behind the shower curtain.

"I'm so tired from standing up. I thought she'd hear me sit down."

Jane grabs my arm, leaning on me. I help her climb out of the tub.

"I tried to disappear, but I couldn't. You should've told me that she could see me."

"I didn't know that she could. I'm sorry. I thought it would be fine."

She sits down on the bathroom floor. She leans against the wall.

"You have to protect me. I can't do this kind of stuff anymore. I need to know you have my back, or I can't do any of this. I need to know you're going to remember me."

"I will. I'm sorry, Jane."

"No, you're not. You're over it. You're getting over this whole thing."

She shakes and cries out of exhaustion.

CHAPTER 8
Engraftment

After the bone marrow transplant, Jane comes back to the house to recover. She's lying in my bed, attached to her IV and a million other steadily beeping machines. I tried to set up the safest space for her that I could, with plastic wrap hanging from the ceiling, surrounding the bed. I doubt it does much, but I'm doing the best I can to keep her air clean. She looks horrible, the worst she's ever looked. She wears a huge plastic mask over her face, covering her nose and mouth. The plastic mask comes to a point in the center with the filter, like the nose of an animal. She doesn't wear her neon pink wig over her bald head. It sits next to her on the bed, flat, lifeless.

"Maia, you have to check for engraftment."

She says it through her air purifier mask, but it's still somehow clear, only slightly muffled.

"Engraftment?"

Jane's slow to respond. She's tired, and really annoyed.

"Maia, *engraftment*. When the new cells I got take to my bone marrow. It marks the start of my transplant recovery process."

"Oh, yeah. How do I check?"

"You need to analyze my lab results. My neutrophils, my platelets, my hemoglobin."

"Got it. Just a second. I'll be right back."

I walk into the living room and sit down. I put my elbows on the table and hold my head in my hands.

Why is Jane back already? She's clearly nowhere close to being ready to leave the ICU. This isn't my job, to take care of her to this extent. I mean, this transplant was severe. I can administer vancomycin, but I don't know how to do this stuff. What the fuck is a neutrophil?

I can't do this.

I'm going to kill Jane, being responsible for this.

I Google "bone marrow transplant recovery process." I skim around. It says, *The transplant team will watch for engraftment by monitoring your lab reports.* So, where's the team then? Why is it only me?

I go back to the bedroom. Jane lies there, lifeless, her neck in an awkward position against the pillow, like she can't quite keep it up. She talks slowly and sickly, being rude to me.

"A neutrophil is a type of white blood cell . . . you cancer idiot."

"You don't have to be so mean."

"I just feel like you have no idea what's going on with me. Just because you got out easy without a transplant doesn't mean you couldn't have educated yourself on what it would have been like." She pauses, takes a deep breath. "Your friends at the hospital school got transplants. It's the least you could've done, read some articles."

"Stop it, okay? We really can't fight at a time like this. We have to work together. Just help me, please. How do I test your counts?"

She points to the corner of the room where a lab station appears with a bunch of syringes and vials.

"You need to take blood from my central line. You need to look at it under the microscope."

Okay, I can do that. I watched the nurses take blood from my central line a million times. I take a saline and heparin syringe, alcohol wipe, and vial back over to Jane. She pulls up her shirt to her belly, so the red and white central line tubes hang out. I choose blue. I clean it with the alcohol wipe, connect the saline, and shoot it through. Then the heparin.

"Feels okay?" I say.

"Yeah," she says. I remember the feeling, an unnatural thing, to be aware of your veins. I attach an empty vile and pull it back, filling it with Jane's blood. But it doesn't work right. It's not a smooth steady flow like when the nurses did it. Blood barely comes out, and there's a giant air bubble.

"Maia! Look at that! What are you doing?"

"I don't know."

"Come on! This isn't difficult!"

Jane takes the vial from me and pulls her own blood with her weak hand. She transfers it perfectly.

I take the blood to the "lab," the microscope on my desk in the corner of the room. I try to remember everything I can from high school biology. We practiced on these things, didn't we? Shouldn't I have to do something else, like prepare the blood? Aren't there machines it needs to be processed through? There's no way it was really like this when I was in the hospital, when they did my labs. But Jane's telling me that this is the only way, so I have to try. I pour a drop of blood on a square glass piece, cover it with another, put it under the microscope, and pull it into focus like a camera.

My breathing slows while I investigate her blood. It's calming, the way her blood looks, her blood cells on a little square like that, like a picture frame. But I don't know what I'm seeing. I don't know what red blood cells, platelets, or white blood cells are supposed to look like, or how I'm supposed to count them by looking this way. There has to be another instrument, appliance, an instruction manual for real lab scientists. I look around the room. There's nothing.

My phone's ringing on Jane's bedside table. I sit up from the microscope and pull it out of my back pocket. It's the high school.

"I've gotta take this. It's about my application."

"Are you serious? Phone? Right now?" says Jane.

"Just let me deal with it."

I leave Jane alone with the machines. I try to relax before opening the front door.

"Hello?" I answer, stepping out onto the porch. I fold my arms in the cold.

"Hi, this is Susan Reynolds, from St. John High School. Is this Maia?"

"Yes, hi, Susan, thank you for calling."

"I received your resume for the open teaching position. I'd like to schedule an interview with you sometime next week. Does that work for you?"

"That would be great."

"How's Tuesday, at 1:30?"

I take five minutes before going back inside. I sit on the porch and let myself be happy about the possibility of moving forward.

———————————

"Maia! I can't believe you just left me after everything I've just gone through. I can't believe you answered your phone!" says Jane as I walk back in the house.

"It was five minutes. I'm sorry," I say, walking into the bedroom. "I just had to go out for a second."

"Did you check my counts?"

"Yeah, Jane, everything looks good."

I'm lying and she knows it, but what am I supposed to say? That I don't know what's going on? That it's up to her to get better now, that even if I did check and know the status of her transplant, it's not like I could do anything to help her? I'm not a doctor!

I can't tell her, though. I don't want to freak her out, bring her spirits down. I don't want to screw with her mind-body connection.

"Do you want something to eat?"

"Ice chips," she says. Thankfully, I have them ready. I go to the freezer and fill a cup with them. I sit with her on the bed while she chews them, letting it slide, even though it's bad for her teeth.

"I have to go to the bathroom," she says.

I help her get out of bed and walk her through the plastic walls. She leans on my arm. She is the frailest and lightest she's ever been. I wait outside the door while she goes. I hear her urine hit the plastic container, like rain on a tarp. Then the sink goes on. She washes her hands for what feels like half an hour.

"Oh my god. I look terrible," Jane says as she comes out of the bathroom. "I look like a St. Jude's commercial."

As I help her hobble back to bed, I feel my phone buzzing in my pocket again.

"Do you want to watch *Music and Lyrics*?" she asks.

"Yeah," I say, glancing at my phone as she gets settled. It's the school again. "But the TV is in the living room, and you'll be more comfortable here in bed. Let me get my laptop, okay? I'll see if I can find it online."

I know she can hear the front door close. She's going to be so mad, upset that I left again. But I have to answer, don't I? I have to live my life. She's not real—none of this is real. I have to learn this. I have to move forward. It's freezing outside, but I can't feel it anymore. My blood runs through me, hot, afraid.

I miss the call. I take a short walk down the street, waiting for the voicemail.

"Hi, Maia, this is Susan from St. John. I'm so sorry to call again. Could you please send a sample of possible syllabi or courses you've taught before the interview? Thank you."

Shit. Sample syllabi? A course I've taught and designed myself? I don't have that. All I've done is part-time assistant teaching in college.

But I can't think about this now. I have to get back to Jane. She's going to be furious with me for leaving her, for only becoming a teacher after all of this.

I start running back to the house. As I approach my place, I trip and fall to the ground. I get up, worried about my stitches, but that knee is fine; it's the other one that's throbbing. I roll up my jeans and see it bruising immediately. What's my platelet count? Probably amazing compared to Jane's right now. My palms are bleeding, scraped, dirty where I landed on them. But I keep moving forward. I have to get back to her.

I get my computer from the kitchen table and go back into the bedroom, pull back the plastic wrap, and sit on the bed next to Jane.

"Jane, I found it. Sorry that took so long. I guess I left my computer in the car."

"What happened to your hands? Get out of here! Get out! That's going to give me an infection."

"Geez, okay. I'm sorry."

"How could you be so careless?"

I drop the laptop on her bed, but she won't go near it. She acts like it's the most disgusting thing she's ever seen and makes a face at it. I walk to the bathroom, scrubbing my hands in the sink with soap and rubbing them; it stings. I stare at myself in the mirror, tears welling out of pain and stress. *Don't.* I hold them back.

When I go back in, Jane tells me her whole body hurts.

"Get the morphine. It's over by the syringes," she tells me.

"It's really bad for you, Jane. You can get addicted to that stuff."

"You're kidding, right?"

"Not really, no."

"I might not even survive this, given the janky way you're caring for me right now. Give me the morphine."

"Fine."

But I don't know how to. Do I administer it right through her central line? Or do I put it through an IV bag? I just stand there, waiting for her to say something. But she doesn't. Finally, I just pick one.

I do the same process again, clean the central line with the alcohol wipe, the saline, and heparin from the bedside table. Then I push the morphine through, just a little to start. But Jane says that's not enough. I give her half a syringe. Is that too much? I don't know what to do.

After a few minutes, I can see the morphine settle in her. Her whole body relaxes. She closes her eyes.

"Jane? You good?"

"I want to nap now."

"I'm going to Mel's tomorrow, remember?"

"You're still going to go?"

I have to, because none of this is real. No matter how sick she gets, I have to go on and be a regular person. I have to move forward with my life.

I wait for her to fall completely asleep, then check that her heart is still beating.

I change into pajama shorts and a huge T-shirt, put a bandana in my hair, and imagine my escape from this. I sit on the bathroom floor with a sharp pair of eyebrow scissors and look at the bandage on my knee. I rip it off in one clear rip. It hurts, pulls out all the hairs I haven't been able to shave. Then I take the stitches out myself, one by one. Eight little pieces of black string fall to the floor.

CHAPTER 9
Automobile

I stand in front of the car with its hood up, mine up too. I look into the engine, into the bones of my machine. Metal tubes topped with yellow and red caps; corrosion sits shameless. Each part connects to another, says something, speaks. I see it all, this body. But I don't understand any of it.

I unscrew the oil, wipe it, test it. I fill it up, in the white paper filter. I take care of this body. I think, *Feels cold, honey?* "Just a bit," says machine. I get in, start the ignition, go forward, flip around, ditching Jane for the first time. In this car, I have a new body, and I must use it. I drive to the freeway, out and away from this city. It is a choice in time, to move a body forward, to move a body outward.

I fly down the freeway at unbelievable pace, like in the dream I had in kindergarten, a flight so real I thought it was actually happening. Wheels churn me forward. Here, in this body, I am not allowed to be stagnant. My new body moves and forgets everything from before, every exit, every car beside it. I hear nothing but air bash into my ears. Driving to the Bay, I think about the bodies I want to be—Maserati, Lamborghini, Pagani Huayra. I don't think about where I'd be if I drove just an hour more. I don't think about what's past Mel's house in Oakland—the Lucile Packard Children's Hospital. I don't imagine my parents on the same freeway as I am right now, driving back and forth, paying the same toll, FasTrak. I only imagine Oakland, with my old friend in her new house and new job and new life with her new boyfriend. I want to remember nothing but my freedom, and the imprisonment my parents must have felt on this drive to see my body in an auto shop, to frantically wipe me of my grease.

———————————

It takes me fifteen minutes to find parking on Mel's street, but it's a good thing. It gives me time to settle my nerves, nerves of seeing a life I'm jealous of, nerves of my actions, nerves that I'll destroy a friendship like I have once before. I'm nervous for an abrupt shift in her mood, like in high school, for my inability to figure out what I said or did wrong. I call her in the car like I told her I would. I drive up and down the streets, avoiding the wide-open curb blocked for street cleaning.

"You're early," she says, picking up the phone, her voice blasting through my car speaker. I turn it down. "I'm not ready. I'm still cleaning up. The place is a mess."

"It's fine, seriously. Don't clean for me."

On the third lap, I find an open spot. I suck at parallel parking. It takes me a minute. When I finally get it right, I take my bag out of the trunk and look at my phone, checking the house number again. I walk down a block, turn left. She lives in one side of a brown house. Mel must've seen me walking up from the window. She opens the door before I knock.

"Maia!"

We hug.

"I'm so excited to be here."

"Let me give you a mini tour."

Mel's place is like mine but better. Somehow, while apart, we grew into the same style. The house is small, but open, colorful. There are plants everywhere, and a big comfortable couch, pretty blankets, pillows. The kitchen has white and blue tile, an old-fashioned sink and appliances, Meyer's soap. Quaint. Nontoxic. There are different types of cut flowers in a vase on the kitchen table. The main difference between her place and mine: instead of Jane, there's a boyfriend in the bedroom.

"Hey, Maia," Jay says, walking out and giving me a hug. He goes over to Mel, kisses her quickly.

"Going back to work?" she says.

"Yeah, but I'll see you guys later."

I want what they have, a bond, an ability to talk about the *real*. I'm jealous of the way in which they probably sat on that couch the night before, talked about my body and what Mel and I went through as children. My body is something they get to share, listen, make sense of. Yet it is still a body I cannot.

Jay leaves, and Mel and I sit at the kitchen table together. She gets me a glass of water.

"I can't believe he has to work so much."

"Yeah, because of tax season, he's been at the office every night, basically, and Saturdays."

"Accountant life!" I say in a nerdy tone.

"Seriously."

I sip my water.

"I'm so glad you're here," she says again.

"Me too," I say, setting the glass down. "I'm excited for tonight. Where are we going?"

"Well, we could go to a few bars this afternoon that are fun for drinks. Then we can get dinner afterwards. I have a few places I think you would like."

"Awesome. Should we get ready to go now, then? What should we wear?"

"I was thinking something kinda cute, not fancy though."

We go into her room. I rummage through my overnight bag,

realizing what I brought for the occasion probably isn't going to work.

Mel comes out of her closet in a yellow halter top, buttoning up high-waisted jeans.

"You look awesome," I tell her. She seems way cooler here than she is in Sacramento, and I wonder if I would be too if I left. I show her the boring, black long-sleeved T-shirt I brought. "I'm definitely going to need to borrow something."

"Try on whatever you want."

I look through her closet as she puts on minimal Glossier makeup at the vanity. I don't dare go near her pants or skirts, knowing my flat wall of an ass could never fill them. I stop on a cropped polo shirt.

"That would be cute on you."

I put it on, and Mel and I look in the mirror together. I turn side to side, but it only gets worse. My boobs look massive and square, my shoulders look huge, and the soft hair on my Greek stomach is totally visible.

"Ew," I say.

I want to try on more of her clothes, her trendy, Urban Outfitters-ish, small-chested, decently-sized-butt clothes. Her new best friend can wear them too. I looked at her Instagram. The only clothes that look good on me will look bad on both of them, and vice versa. I put the shirt I brought on.

"Mind if I borrow this?" I ask, pointing to a blush in her makeup bag.

"Go ahead."

I give myself a blood transfusion of color from the plastic container. Red rises in my cheeks. I start putting on mascara, leaning closer to the mirror.

"Throwback to when my eyelashes fell out because my blood cells ate each other," I say.

"Geez, Maia, don't say that." But she laughs for a second, and so do I.

Then tears start to well in her eyes.

"Mel, stop. I'm serious. We can't go there. We have to just have a fun night together, being old like this, being young."

"I know, you're right."

She laughs and sniffles at the same time.

"I'm gonna call our Lyft," she says, leaving the room. I continue applying mascara, but it's pointless. My eyes fill too. My vision blurs. My eyes sting.

———————

At the second bar, we order a round of margaritas. We take a look at the menu, which seems good, and decide to eat here instead of going somewhere else. I'm relieved. I need to get something in my stomach before I get plastered from low alcohol tolerance. We order mac and cheese and chicken wings.

It feels good, to be out like this, in some cool wooden bar, like a barn, with Basquiat-esque art on the walls and pop music I've never heard before. I like the way my body feels here. I feel like a nobody again, like I was in New York City. Except it's different now. I'm a *nobody* beside a person who knows *everybody* I am.

"How's your book going?" Mel asks.

"It's dumb."

"Come on."

"I hate it. I'm so embarrassed by my writing, honestly."

"You're writing a book! It's so cool. Honestly, I've felt jealous of you for making art. You're doing this writing thing that you love."

"But you have such a cool life here. I'm just in our hometown doing nothing."

"I'm sure you do more than you give yourself credit for," she says, scooping some mac and cheese onto her fork. "You know, it's kind of cool the way we're both doing exactly what we said we would as kids."

"What do you mean?" I ask.

"You always said you wanted to write your cancer book, and I said I would go into mental health and try to open my own clinic. I'm obviously not there yet, but I'm working toward it."

"I don't feel like I need to write that cancer book anymore."

Mel doesn't believe me.

"Really?"

"I don't know."

"It seems like you're telling the cancer story a bit through your uncle, as least from the chapter you let me read."

"That's the only chapter where I talk about cancer, though. The rest is only gonna be about him."

When the food arrives, Mel is talking about some of the patients at her clinic.

"Their problems can be really overwhelming. They've had really bad shit happen to them. I've had a relatively easy life."

"But your best friend got cancer," I say.

The waitress comes to refill our waters. We pause awkwardly, waiting for her to finish pouring.

"It happened to you, though, not to me."

"I think this is a problem in society, with the community around sick people. Their trauma is totally overlooked. I mean, no one asks my sisters or parents how they feel about it anymore, like ever."

Back at the house, Mel and I sit at the kitchen table with Jay. Empty Heineken bottles surround us.

"Tahoe?"

"Big Sur?"

"Too cold."

"We'll figure out somewhere to go. It would be fun."

Mel and I tell Jay about going to Tahoe as kids, and other stories from childhood. We talk about fighting with Kenzie Renwald and Julia Dixon, making rap videos, and getting ice cream at Vic's. We talk about eating insane amounts of cheese on top of pasta at her house, making cookies, and defending Mr. Joseph when everyone else thought he was a mean teacher. Neither of us bring up anything from when I was sick.

"How is work?" Jay asks me.

"Oh, I quit my job a few months ago. I'm actually working on writing a book right now."

"Really? About what?"

"It's about the way drowning relates to illness," I say, looking at Mel for confirmation, finally admitting that maybe I am writing a cancer book. But that explanation doesn't feel right coming out of my mouth. "Mel told you I used to have cancer, right?"

"Yeah, what kind was it again?"

"Leukemia."

I'm surprised they didn't talk about me more before I got here, about my writing, about my cancer. I'm embarrassed to realize that they have other things going on, that my body isn't the center of everyone's attention.

I keep talking.

"Drowning is a good way to describe how I felt when I was sick, though. You're just trying, every day, to get enough air. Some people come up, and some people stay down."

They both nod and drink.

"Oh my gosh, I'm so intense. Sorry, everyone. I'm gonna shut up now."

"It's fine, Maia," says Mel. She makes eye contact with Jay. I think she's trying to tell him she's had enough of the topic. He doesn't get it.

"Have you seen the movie *Five Feet Apart*?" he asks.

"Oh, God, gross," I say.

"I kind of liked it. They do the drowning thing too."

———

The next morning, I'm hungover and tired, though I thought I slept well on their couch. I shouldn't have had so much to drink. It's not good for my heart. I wake up before Mel, like I always did when we were kids. I stare up at the ceiling and wait, running through every conversation from the night before in my head. Did I say anything I shouldn't have? We had fun, right? Finally, I hear a toilet flush, and Mel comes in to check on me. I make room, and she sits down on the couch with me. Jay takes the chair across from us a few minutes later. We all sit in our pajamas. Their tall cacti surround us. We don't say much. Everyone seems pretty out of it. Is it because we're tired from drinking? Or is it because Mel is upset with me? I probably did do something wrong.

We have breakfast, orange juice with scrambled eggs and avocados from their tree in the backyard. I barely help. They do everything together. We sit at the kitchen table and eat, and then Jay has to go to work. He gets ready, and I say bye to him and sit with Mel a while longer. She insists on doing all the dishes. I want to tell her she doesn't have to take care of me.

I get my things together. She walks me to my car down the block.

"Thanks for letting me stay."

"I'm so glad you could come."

I put my bag in the trunk.

"It's really nice to be so close again," she says.

I agree, but I think I'd have to get cancer again for it to ever be the same.

"I don't want to be weird or, like, take it from you, but the fact that you're writing about cancer is really therapeutic for me. It's nice to see everything you went through becoming something."

"No, don't worry; I love hearing that. It's been like that for me too."

I start the car and move forward, past the big, spaced-out houses, trees. I feel terribly hungover, like I'm going to throw up. I head past the lake, onto the bumpy street, toward the freeway. I sweat in the car getting on the on-ramp. I'm hot. My thighs stick to the seat.

I think I lied about writing being therapeutic. It isn't like that yet, but someday it will be. I'll write and talk about cancer until I've solved it, resolved it. Until cancer becomes worth it. In a book, my body will be cancer-free forever. How could that not be therapy?

I lean over and open the glove box. There it is—my manuscript. It's a book about my dead uncle and his body that drowned. It's a book about what it means to not come up for air.

But my story is encompassing his. I take the next exit. I pull over into the parking lot of a coffee shop. I let my notes and ideas about my childhood life take over his crinkled cover page. My childhood blood pours onto his pages like a river, onto an old book I wrote about somebody else.

CHAPTER 10

Neon Jane

On the way home, I stop at the Greek Orthodox church on Alhambra Boulevard, the white building with the stained glass icons across from the McKinley Park Library. When I was a kid, my sisters and I would wait in the communion line in black patent leather shoes to drink the blood of Jesus Christ out of a goblet, and then eat the body, the holy bread baked by the old Greek ladies. At Greek church, everybody takes communion from the same wine goblet, but you don't get sick—you don't pass diseases. You're drinking the blood of Jesus Christ. It's special. You even drink it when you're a baby. Your mom holds you up, and the priest asks you, "Servant of God?" and you're supposed to tell him your name, but you're a baby, so your mom says it for you. Then the priest shoves the spoon in your tiny baby mouth. You cry, but it disappears. As a baby, you realize, *The blood of Jesus disappears inside of me.* You learn that—as terrible as it seems to drink a nasty mixture everyone else in the entire church has drank out of—it sort of tastes good, feels good, the way it sinks into your tongue, the way it takes you on.

I wait in line to put a dollar in the wooden donation box and light a tall candle for my uncle Jason, like my mom used to do back when we still went to this church regularly. I tell him, "I'm sorry for taking over your book." I push the bottom of the candle deep into the sand next to the other dead people, all lit up and flickering, reminding us that they still exist, that they're still watching. I line up with the other Greeks in their dark outfits and black flats, realizing now how severely underdressed I am. I follow them into the church, overcome by incense. The hidden chorus greets me with an eerie "*kyrie, eléison*" as I remember walking down through this dim church in my neon-pink wig, holding my mother's hand. It was my first time back at Greek church since treatment. I was embarrassed and scared to wear a neon pink wig in a holy place like this, but my mom was there. She led me. The priest looked up at me from the alter. He recognized me, and he nodded.

In the communion line, my sisters and I didn't fight. No one shoved me. I scratched my scalp under my pink wig, and then I was frozen, afraid, standing at the front of the line. It was just me and the priest, in his long, white outfit and golden cross around his neck.

"Servant of God?" he asked.

I stood there and stared at him.

"Maia," my mother said behind me. "Tell him your name, honey."

I said my name, but it didn't sound right coming out of my mouth anymore. It sounded like the name of somebody else, like somebody's childhood nickname. Cancer had left me a physically and mentally different person. I followed my family in a straight line and sat down for prayer, on the back right. I couldn't pray. I just sat there, staring off into space, like I am right now. I find it difficult to pray in churches.

———

When I get home, I throw my manuscript on the kitchen table and walk through the plastic curtains I made for Jane's ICU. She's asleep. The pink wig has fallen off her head, messy and tangled, peeking out from the orange comforter. The air purifier mask sits on the bedside table next to her.

Jane has a lot of color in her cheeks for being by herself all night.

She looks like engraftment has begun, like she's healing, glowing. Seeing her like this makes me surrender to her all over again, like I have so many times before. I sit next to her on the bed and put my hands on her back gently, careful not to wake her up.

I close my eyes and breathe. I try to channel the strength of my uncle Jason. "If you hear me, show me a sign," I whisper to him. He doesn't show. He wants me to know I'm on my own.

I close my eyes and send all the energy I have through the palms of my hands. I ask Jane's body to heal, to grow up, to be safe and alive. I ask her to never relapse. I pray energy through my hands and deep into her blood cells, and I ask them all, one by one, to never do what they've done ever again. I stay next to her a while longer, trying to find a way to make this beautiful.

Jane starts to roll over, waking up.

"Maia?" she says in a tired whisper. She feels her cold, bald head and starts to look for her wig. I pull it from the covers and put the synthetic strands back into place for her.

"I'm sorry that I went on the trip to Mel's," I say, looking into Jane's tired eyes.

"I was mad at first," she says quietly, propping herself up on her elbows, still a bit dazed. "But I get it. I would probably want a break from all this, too." She gestures around the room, to all the medical equipment.

"Have you been okay?"

"Yeah. I think I'm pretty good at taking care of myself."

"Yeah?"

"Yeah," Jane says.

Tears start to well in her eyes. I want to hug her, but I can't. I haven't showered since yesterday morning and don't know her cell counts.

"What's that?" I say, pointing to a Ziplock bag of buttons on the orange bedspread.

"I was disinfecting those for art therapy."

"I remember that exercise. It's called 'Holding it Together,' right?"

"Yeah. We can play. But you need to go get cleaned up first, and probably eat something. You don't look so good. And can you get the glue gun?"

———————

I go to the kitchen, disinfect the counters, and peel a banana. I take the quickest shower in the world. I wrap myself in a clean robe and twist the towel around the hair on top of my head.

I go back to the bedroom with a chair from the kitchen and plug in the hot glue gun. Jane squirts sanitizer into my hands, and we begin the game, the art therapy.

Jane digs through the bag of two hundred disinfected buttons from the Rec Center. There are so many different colors, shapes, and sizes. It's hard for her to choose one. She wants something that speaks to her. She doesn't want to force it.

She picks a black button in the shape of a triangle. I put a dot of glue on the paper for her, and she sticks the triangle button down quickly. She writes: *There are three parts of me: the before, during, and after.*

"What do you mean?" I ask.

"I mean there's a before, during, and after cancer version of myself, though I haven't gotten to the after cancer one yet."

I know exactly what she means. I run my finger along the sides of the button. I try to push her further.

"Don't forget the edges," I tell her.

"The edges?"

"The places where you're both, where you transition. The places that connect those three parts of you."

"Cancer hippie much?" Jane smiles.

We laugh together.

"Sounds like you're becoming one too now."

"No way."

She sifts through the button bag again, picking a wooden one with a yellow flower painted across it.

"Okay, I think this one represents how it feels to be haunted by you, Maia," she says.

"Haunted by me?"

"Yeah, sorry. Does that hurt your feelings?"

"No. It's okay."

She pauses.

"I mean that there's pressure on me to get better for my future self so she can grow up and achieve everything she wants to."

She writes her caption and smiles at me, like she knows something she shouldn't.

"Why do you call me Jane, anyways?"

I become acutely aware of the heart in my chest.

"It can be very scary to write about yourself."

She nods, in acknowledgment, but she doesn't really get it. She thinks she's stronger than me, that she'd never need another character.

She picks a few more buttons, and then we start *Music and Lyrics* on my laptop on the bed. During the movie, I clean her central line with saline solution and heparin. I clean the insertion sight with the orange scented wipes. As she lies there, eyes locked on the movie, I gently scrub the tiny hole in Jane's chest. I clean the white tube shooting through it, hanging on with purple stitching, about to break lose.

Jane's asleep by the time the credits roll. I turn the movie off and clean the entire room. Clorox wipes touch every surface, somehow an acceptable toxicity in my house. I wipe down the machines, medicine bottles, the bedside table, the cover of Jane's diary, the dresser knob handles, the bathroom door handle.

I take a break. I close the curtains and lie on the bed, staring at the corner of the ceiling where the wall meets the window—an opening into my home, my body. I doze in and out of sleep next to Jane.

I dream that I am sitting on the sidewalk outside the Lucile Packard Children's Hospital. Jane is older, sixteen or seventeen. Her hair is short, a brown bob. Edgy. We watch the cars go by on Welch Road.

"You're not going to get cancer again," she tells me, leaning back on her palms.

"I know that," I say.

"No, you don't."

I don't say anything. I stare down the road.

"I used to think I'd get cancer again someday after this too," Jane goes on, retying her dirty black Converse high-tops. "But I don't anymore."

"Why not?"

"I just grew out of it. Or maybe, I grew into it. Or I outgrew you."

"But that's impossible."

"I can't do this anymore, stew in it, you know. I want to own it, cancer, from this point on in life."

"But you don't have a life. I mean, you're me, but different—"

"Well, I don't want to be you anymore; I don't want to be your extension. I want to be real, to grow up, to age, to be my own person. I want to be free of cancer. I want to be cancer-free."

"But . . . you protect me," I say, looking down, scratching my head.

"But no one can protect you."

We sit silently for a minute, watching the visitors pull into the hospital driveway, checking in with the old man at the gate.

Teenage Jane looks at me, shaking her head.

"Why are you still wearing that thing anyways?"

"Wearing what?" I say, feeling confused.

"The pink wig, you idiot."

Jane takes my neon-pink wig off. We watch my hair unroll and unroll and unroll for miles down the street.